A Star in a Storm

Peter J. Mauro

About the Author

Peter J. Mauro was born in 1940 in South Philadelphia to Gennaro and Marie Mauro. Pete had Twin sisters 5 years younger than him, and at the age of 17, he unexpectedly lost his father, forcing him to become much more responsible at an early age. Pete earned an Associates Degree in Mechanical Design from Temple University while working in his family's food market and helping take care of his mother and two sisters.

Pete married his wife of 53 years, Maryann (nee Perri) in 1969, where through the 1970's they had two children and moved to South Jersey. Along the way he started his career at Amtrak where he retired after 30 years in 2002. Having had part time jobs throughout his career, sometimes two-to-three on top of his full-time job to help raise his family, Pete was no stranger to hard work, dedication, and perseverance. Whether it was using his degree or just working extra hours at a gas station, Pete was determined to give his kids a better life. So, it was no surprise that upon retirement Pete took on various part time jobs along the way, delivering car parts, driving for rental car companies, or just helping their sons in their businesses.

Throughout his career, all his jobs, and all the used cars that helped him through them, Pete never forgot to prioritize the most important things in his life: his wife, his kids, and his friends. He also found time for his own passions: writing music, singing opera, and of course being Italian, eating well.

Pete and Maryann still reside in their forever home in South Jersey, have two sons and two daughters-in-laws, seven grandchildren, and three great grandchildren. The most prolific characteristic they have passed onto to them all is the importance of friendship, including the characteristics that make a great friend. Those very characteristics, whether used in everyday life, at work, with a spouse, our kids, and even strangers are what helped define success for Pete, Maryann, and their family. Both Pete and his wife Maryann have long standing friendships to this very day. These friendships were foundationally built from childhood, with their closest bunch of friends in their lives from as early as four years old. To this day, those friends (those that are still alive) still get together regularly to play cards, eat, laugh, tell stories, and share in their ups and downs in life. It is through the deep friendships that Pete has nurtured over his 82 years on earth that formed the inspiration for this book.

Contents

Part I
Chapter 1
Damon and Jimmy

Saturdays were usually pleasant for Damon Cittone. No work, sleep, relaxing, daydreaming. Thinking about Friday night and planning the rest of the weekend. However, there was still volunteer work at church, the shelter, the hospital and with the disabled seniors that lived next door to his friend Mike and the one next to Annie a block away. This Saturday was cleanup day at his church where a few volunteers swept, mopped, dusted, and did odd fix up jobs at the church's properties.

Even if there was no pay, there was always something good cooking in the rectory kitchen, and this day was no exception. He could smell the stuffed peppers as he entered the rectory building. He and the other two volunteers worked hard and quickly since they knew it was chow time when the building was clean. That's why it was the last one to be done. The meal was enjoyed by the helpers, priests and the cook, and as they cleared dishes and cleaned up, he was alone with the pastor of the parish. Damon told him some personal things; it's not a confession, it's a discussion. Father Albert believes in confession, but he often finds the informal chat can help more than the formal way of a confession box in certain cases.

Damon told the priest about shortcomings. Father suggested prayer and keeping occupied with things that will help mind, body and soul. The Priest noticed this young man in the neighborhood speaking to and helping people occasionally. He's told he has a knack for assisting others. Priest says keep it up. Damon does so on good days. For now, good days outnumber bad.

Next day, Damon was sitting on the step of his home outside and the priest drove by. He was in a hurry to give last rites to a critically ill woman in the hospital. Holy man thinks he knows fastest route to dying person. But not sure. He asks Damon for directions. Damon has a pen on him and tells the priest a shortcut to St. Luke's Memorial Hospital by writing on the priest's hand and tells him to soap it soon after. The Priest makes it to an elderly woman with a fatal head wound from a fall downstairs minutes before she expires. She just has time to pray with the Holy man and falls asleep seconds later. She doesn't wake up. Priest thanks God, fate, luck and Damon to himself. On the way back to his rectory, Father O'Brien brings Damon a necklace with a cross to wear on his neck and tells him the story of what occurred. Damon felt good. Another one of the good days.

James Callahan was one policeman assigned to the Third Police District, which covered most of Damon's neighborhood in South Hazelton, PA. Officer Callahan, or "Jimmy Cal," helped more than a few young people stay out of real trouble by mentoring, assisting with food parcels or steering teens away from drug, sex and gang dominated sections of his district. It worked more than half the time and when guidance didn't sink into their young brains, he did his best to scare the hard cases with true tales of gang violence to those inside and outside most gangs, and especially detailing prison life as it applies to youngsters just entering the system. Jimmy always described the pain endured by those involved in these situations, be it physical, mental, emotional, or all of the above.

When he did hit stubborn cases, he made required arrests and drove the young suspects past well-known high-crime areas, and made sure someone witnessed what happens when you're caught by Jimmy Cal. The officer felt he did his best in his job using this method, and most neighbors agreed and appreciated his efforts toward their neighborhoods and their youngsters.

Damon was one of those well aware of the cops' presence and the quite favorable job he performed deterring as much crime as he, in fact, did. They knew each other by word of mouth in their respective neighborhoods. Damon was the young man that helped homeless, and Jimmy was the cop to go to before little trouble became too hot to handle. The policeman would speak with Damon when the young man would stop and watch a couple innings of softball that the officer helped coach at the Cay Park a few blocks from Damon's house. On one occasion, he learned the officer was married with two kids, and he adored his family. Sometimes they would come to the games and watch dad coach. Jimmy's wife was quite attractive and sociable, and his daughter of three adored her dad. His two-year-old son kept calling "daddy, daddy," through most of the game and enjoyed the people running and throwing and hitting the ball. He kept trying to run onto the field, but his mother kept in tow. By talking to spectators at the games, Damon learned an unpleasant fact; the policeman's son was ill.

The two-year-old child had a small tumor near his brain, which was difficult to operate on. For the time being, two M.D.'s agreed that it was not presently malignant, and with any luck it may never be so.
If it ever became necessary to remove this growth, it would be quite costly and not fully covered by many insurance plans. Opinions varied regarding how much time the youngster would have if malignancy occurred. But all agreed that if this unfortunate event came to pass, time would be of the essence.

The officer coach came over to the family in the bleachers for about a minute during the game. He spoke briefly to his wife about the game, smiled at his daughter, and rubbed his son's head. Damon took careful notice of Jimmy Cal's eyes when the officer looked at his son. They were smiling, but worried. His expression made a powerful impression on Damon Cittone. He wouldn't soon forget it.

Chapter 2
Linda, Jimmy's kid, and a neighbor

Next day on the bus ride coming home from work, Damon was again picturing Jimmy Cal and his son, and the complex look on Jimmy's face, when he noticed a car with a flat that was being tended to by a young girl. He immediately signaled he wanted off; and did so half a block from the unlucky driver. What especially grabbed Damon's attention was the location of the vehicle regarding oncoming traffic; it was entirely too close. The young man trotted to the site, half-screaming to the girl to get out of the path of traffic. Seconds later, he was on the scene, quickly stating his concern for her safety and offered to push her auto as far onto the shoulder as possible. Because of the crown in the road, it was a downhill push, and easier than it appeared once the wheels started rolling. This accomplished, he figured why not change the tire and mount the spare? He quickly removed three of the nuts but had no luck with the last two. The driver witnessed this and put her hands next to his, and they both pushed on the wrench. No movement. The girl quickly got a hammer from under her driver's seat and whacked and got some rotation and tried increasingly more until it was loose. Repeating this on the last nut, the flat was removed. Damon installed the spare and was thanked with a kiss on the cheek by the pretty driver. "I owe you a favor," she smiled. Smiling back, the young man asked for a ride home. She agreed. "Just don't hit me with your hammer," Damon blurted out seriously. They both laughed.

Outside his home, he requested her phone number in case he ever gets a flat. She had no phone but gave the work number and home address. They made a tentative date for lunch. She offers to treat. Damon says next time. "Confident aren't we." Realizing what he said, Damn countered with, "Just in case you need help with another flat...battery...starter...radio..." "Stop it," she laughed. Damon joined in. They were loud laughers. When they were quiet again, he noticed a certain look from her. Tells her his name is Damon. She says, "I'm Linda." He feels good. Another good day.

That evening he goes out drinking. Wants to extend all good days as far as possible. Gets tipsy only and drives home. Finishes night with an old pastime, B.I.B. (Bombed in Bed). Sleeps well. Two days later, Damon takes Linda to lunch. All is well. Some things in common. Some not. Offers to take her to a local baseball game. She agrees. However, she says her favorite game to watch live is hockey. He makes mental note of this. The young man knows hockey is not cheap. Next day, they cheer through most of the game and hug each other when the home team scores the winning run at the end of the game. They enjoy the brief embrace. He thinks they want the same thing. Damon takes her home.

They kiss passionately for a couple of minutes till her mother wakes up. Her mother is particular about young guys dating her daughter. Girl knows it's too late at night to argue. Tells Damon she must go. Says they'll be alone soon enough. Damon is half satisfied. Thinks to himself he'll know what to do when he passes the neighborhood whore's house depending on his horniness at that time.

Damon loved sex, so meeting the neighborhood pro was inevitable. He first saw her on her step, taking money from a man that just didn't seem to be her type. The man left while she remained outside her door, where Damon innocently inquired what her business was. "I sell," she said sternly. "What do you sell?" inquired the young man. "What do you need?" she laughed. "Ha-ha" scratching between the fleshy shapely legs hidden in flesh-colored tight slacks. Damon understood, saying, "I need what you have," hugging her around her shoulders. "Not so fast slick," retorted the girl sternly, pushing him away. "What are you, John Law, without the uniform?" "What a cop? No way!" claimed the youngster. "Prove it!" shouted the girl. 'How?" he asked. "Who do you know?" He mentioned his good friend Mike, the priest, and his barber. "Call them," she said. "They might be sleeping," he claimed. "And you might be leaving in about five seconds if you don't." Damon called Mike, found out he and this businesswoman knew each other, and Mike described Damon to her by phone, saying they were good friends, and he was no more a cop than Mike was. She admitted Damon inside and he finished his business. He visited her occasionally after that first meeting.

So, it was natural for him to ring her bell this particular night after leaving Linda's house. As usual, he was admitted, paid her with his customary tip (he thought it much better to tip beforehand for obvious reasons) and had his fun. He then felt better and relaxed with her on the bed for a short while. He softly asked her, "Why are you a prostitute?" She smiles and whispers in his ear, "cause I'm not a rock star." Asks why she can't get a job. She claims she has no resume. He questions her, makes notes and makes rough copy for her. Tells her get it printed and get it to job listings in newspaper. Two weeks later, Annie the pro gets a call from diner to interview for a waitress job. She catches the bus to the job interview and gets the job. She uses her long-learned charming techniques to receive nice tips from satisfied customers, especially men. Eventually, she prostitutes less and waitresses more until only waitressing is her occupation.

But this was not the only favor Damon did for her. Prior to her food serving career, while she was still selling her God-given gifts, the young man advised her on her price structure. When he finished, she was convinced he was correct in advising her to raise all prices, considering her looks, local competition, and the rather distant location of her nearest competitor. She did so, and she prospered. These increases were an immense help in buying waitress uniforms, outer wear and shoes required for her new profession. Damon often wondered if she ever returned to her former profession, even if only once in a while. He knew he kept seeing her at the diner, but if she repeated, it could only be very seldom. He doubted it, but if she did, Damon was positive she was receiving a good bit more than she charged when they first met, even if Annie was now only a part time peddler of her God-given gifts since she started waitressing at the town diner.

Damon figured Jimmy Cal must know about Annie the prostitute, since she lived and operated in his portion of his police district and nothing much escaped Jimmy C's eyes. He knew from personal experience Annie was almost eccentric when it came to the cleanliness of her clientele. You had to wash with her special soap any portion of your body that contacted her. Even if you remained dressed during your act, at least face, hands, neck and ears better be scrubbed. Naturally, nothing happened without contraceptives. And if you looked or smelled dirty when she answered the doorbell, no chance would you be admitted, regardless of how many hundreds you showed her. She barely even touched the money she received. She eyed both sides of a bill held by a client up to a light, touched the edge of the bill verifying it was one piece of paper, and told you to drop it in an empty cigar box which she swiftly secreted to another room while customers anxiously awaited her re-appearance and their gratification.

What chance was there that Jimmy Cal didn't know of these cleaning eccentrics? Not much, thought Damon. What was more to the point is that Jimmy most likely let Annie practice her trade because of these procedures. Anyway, Jimmy Cal had bigger fish to fry, and this kept him quite busy. Guiding youngsters towards a relatively safe and happy life and away from drugs, gangs, and crime was more urgent than chasing the cleanest whore in creation.

Previously, when seeing Jimmy on the street, the two would exchange greetings, speak briefly and soon depart. A day after his last visit with Annie, Damon saw Jimmy leaving a corner he patrolled and strode up to him and asked if he had time for a quick coffee and donut at a fast-food coffee shop across the street.

He wanted to know about Jimmy, his work, family, and troubles. Even if he was curious about Jimmy C's views on

Annie, he didn't broach the subject. Anyway, Damon felt sure his analysis of Jimmy's opinion of the girl hit the nail on the head the first time. His present purpose was for the two of them to get to know a little about each other, hang out sometimes, play ball, whatever. On this particular day, they happened to be walking toward each other, each giving a wave and Damon asking just loud enough, "Hey Jimmy, how 'bout a coffee and donut?" while pointing across the street at the little shop. The policeman nodded his head, and they both headed for the eatery.

After exchanging pleasantries, Damon briefly relates his life story. He mentions his job, his mother who was widowed for some years back, his new girl he just met, his charity work and some of his friends. Damon enquires about Jimmy, his job, his family, and his interests. "I have a great family," beams Jimmy, "And I'm thankful for them every day. My son is ill with a growth in his head, but the doctors say it's benign at present and we check it every three months. It causes little Jimmy some unconventional behavior, but this is not an issue yet. We'll see how he is when he's old enough for school. Meanwhile, we all love each other. What more can I ask? We live, play, and pray together. You know, there's an old saying, Damon," smiled Jimmy C., "It's not the cards you're dealt, it's how you play the hand." "Amen," said Damon, nodding his head twice.

Shortly they noted the time, exchanged phone numbers and promised to get together when time permitted. Damon tried paying the bill but was halted by Jimmy. "Next time you get it Damon," insisted the officer, pulling out a rather thick roll of bills. "A lot for a cop," thought Damon. Guess he pays all his house bills in cash.

Chapter 3
Facing the truth and advising a youth

There were 106 employees at M.A. Clinton Inc. in 1963. The firm provided engineering, construction, and land services for numerous clients in the Northeastern U.S. It was a good company to work for with the fringe benefits, salary structure and various amenities. Damon Cittone was in his fifth year there and felt he knew five times more about design than when he first started. He was good enough then but didn't grasp concepts quickly. Only eventually. But his drawings were neat and conveyed all necessary info to successfully construct all components he designed. Now he was much faster and often spent only half the effort to complete double the amount of work, which had as much quality as those that worked at Clinton much longer.

It was a standing joke that when a project proved quite difficult to solve and complete, they "should show it to Damon. He's lazy enough to find the easiest way to do it." This was an exaggeration, of course, but Damon was known and respected in the company and was on his way to his second promotion.

The young man just completed his portion of a project successfully and was studying his next job when he was paged into the chief engineer's office. He's hopeful this meeting will result in his raise and new title. He respected Frank A. Clinton Jr. as a knowledgeable engineer and technician and a good man and fair person. Damon thought it quite probable that he would be in a similar position even if he wasn't the owner's nephew. Frank started 25 years ago as an engineer in-training and consistently solved difficult problems in design engineering and knew almost always which personnel to utilize for each specific portion of a project. He got the most out of each and often encouraged many who thought themselves not up to their assignment to push and think a little extra towards a correct conclusion of their respective jobs. Frank did this not only by conveying engineering principles but also by teaching and by practical examples. Young Damon would know he deserved a promotion if this man gave him one. "Come in Damon, and have a seat and I'll be with you shortly," said the engineer as the young man appeared in his doorway. Damon waited. After finishing some paperwork, Frank removed a folder from a drawer, rose, stretched, and started pacing in his office while studying the folder's contents.

Thirty seconds elapsed when the executive smiled and joked, "So you think you deserve a raise, ay?" Damon smiles back silently. "Seriously," continued the elder one, "your work is more than satisfactory. It's very good. Not excellent, because then you would get my job. But well enough for a promotion. There's just one thing I must discuss with you beforehand. As I said, your jobs are on the mark, but in the last month or so, your timeliness seems to have become a problem matter. I've observed you from time to time. Do you daydream, son?" The youngster's stomach tightened. Damon knew from previous occasions that this was a signal that the speaker had hit the nail on the head.

He did not want to lie but couldn't blatantly admit to his mind floating sometimes on a sea of fantasy and make-believe, even if it did. Damon thought fast. "I apologize for giving that impression, sir. The truth of the matter is that I met a girl and I think of her when I should not," He half-lied. "I will stop doing so, immediately since you brought it up, and it will not cause any difficulties with any of my future-jobs, I'm sure."

"Is that it?" said the engineer, laughing. "Well, I was young once too. I guess I can understand that." He half yelled, "are you sure that's all it is?" searched the engineer, seriously looking deeply into Damon's eyes. The youngster dared not blink. "That's all," said the young man evenly, knowing this was not a person he could trifle with. Frank held his stare for a few seconds and relented. "Your raise will be reflected in the paycheck following next one. But there is one stipulation. If I feel dreaming is occupying company time on your part, I reserve the right to withdraw said promotion. Agreed?" Damon nodded agreeably.

He rose from his seat, thanked the man, and offered his hand. The engineer shook it and stated truthfully, "I don't just watch you, Damon. I watch everyone. It's my job. Don't take it personally, it's business. Just remember the conversation. By the way," Frank smiled, "you think I'm not watched? Think again, pal. If you pay 2 million a year in salaries, wouldn't you watch those receiving it? Like I said, not personal. Just the real world."

Damon returns to his job location, fully immersing himself in math, mechanics, electrical and structural problems. He would make himself enjoy the job more than usual. He would not give the wrong impression again. He could fight the temptation to fantasize, he had to. The Chief Engineer was correct in his observations of the young employee.

The young man was engulfed with work for the remaining part of the day. He got thru almost 20% of a job that would require about a week and a half to complete. When he finally glanced at the clock, it was coming on 6:30 P.M.

If he hurried, he could catch the next bus home. He made some quick notes for tomorrow, placed his work in his folder, cleared his desk of scrap papers and any clutter and was ready for the following day's work. He moves quickly out of his building and sees a bus less than ½ mile away. So far, a good day.

Damon takes a bus home from work daily. This evening he meets a young boy about 10 years old on the bus seated next to him. He notices a slight tear in his eye and a look of unhappiness on boy's face. He asks the child if he's ill and the boy says he's not, but he has no one to play with in his neighborhood or in his grandmother's area where he goes after school and is coming from now on the bus. Damon suggests the child try to get good at something and let others see you try. "Maybe try to bounce a rubber ball on a brick wall and catch it. Then do it faster until you do it as fast as possible and still catch the thing. Some kid is bound to come by and ask what you're doing. Tell him or her you're practicing coordination and will play ball someday. Bet you they ask if they can try it. This will lead to somebody else coming along asking the same thing. Be friendly with them, but not silly. Trust them a little at a time. More later. Friendships are made in steps, not like instant lemonade. When you have friends, learn when to have fun, when to work, be it homework, chores or what needs doing. Don't waste time. You'll never get back yesterday. Don't say there's nothing to do. This is common with the young. Everything can't be exciting. Brushing teeth is not exciting. It just needs doing. There's always exercise, reading, homework, the library, cleaning your room, staying clean, friends, going for walks, learning all you can while strolling about. You know when to stop learning, son?"

"After school?" asks the child. "No," answers Damon. "When you stop breathing." Boy says, "Thank you, mister, I'll try it." Damon says, "Call me Damon." Child gets off the bus. Damon is content. He's relaxed for the rest of the ride and daydreams about being a movie star. After a few minutes, he catches himself and stops the fantasy. He slept till his street was called.

Chapter 4
A friend, and more advice

Mike Sampson was a good friend to many in his neighborhood and at work, but he was Damon's best friend. They grew up together, had fun, got hurt, got sick, got better and learned the street, about life, about girls and all they absorbed in 2 ½ decades they had been alive. They agreed on much. Mike's favorite point of disagreement regarded adults that daydream. Damon heard that discussion more than once. It may be a bone of contention in later years, but not now. But then, Mike never really saw his buddy at his fantasizing best. Damon hoped he never did, anyway. Damon was now determined to avoid any make-believe thoughts and actions near anyone since his promotion. He wanted to start a new phase in his life.

The two friends usually met once a week for lunch at one of their favorite eateries. Mike worked down a couple blocks from Damon's job at the local high school, where he was an assistant counselor. This might be a temporary position granted by the school board to assist the head counselor with many troubled teens at the secondary school. Sometimes Mike thought he was a babysitter instead of a guidance counselor. His degree in Psychology with a minor in juvenile studies/problems helped prepare him for his role, but no more than the two years he spent at his first job after college at the youth study center as assistant to the officers in charge of non-violent male youth.

For the most part, this was a mild-mannered group, but that factor in no way diminished the problems this company of young boys carried with them. Besides the laziness prevalent in most, there were many with strong tendencies towards drugs, deviant sex, alcohol, gambling, fantasy and either low I.Q.'s or normal or better I.Q.'s but just a general resistance to learning either in the academic section of the center or the skilled and unskilled trades portion of the institution. Mike assisted in both, depending on which had more problems on any given day. Sometimes these kids were so far out that he had to help them wash their hands and face or even shower, blow their noses, shave without bleeding to death or wiping themselves after toilet visits.

He even lobbied for a few hopeless ones to wear incontinence diapers, but that either got a laugh or fell on deaf ears in the administration office. The young assistant helped many, but nowhere near all he attempted to assist. But Mike was satisfied that he did all he could in words and actions for the wide mix of faces that attended the facility.

During lunch, a few days following Damon's raise in pay, he figured he'd treat his buddy to a meal and brag a little about his job status. They had a pleasant lunch during which they spoke of sports, girls, work and what they expected of themselves in the coming years. Mike thought he wanted to be head counselor at the school, but he would see how this present position worked out before putting his eggs in one basket. Damon almost tripped into one of his delusions of grandeur but held his tongue and simply stated he wished to achieve success where he was and continue to rise at his company. After lunch, they made plans for the next volunteer job, parted, and returned to their respective places of employment.

While Damon was strolling towards work, he saw an elderly man fishing on the bridge that crossed Canton Creek, which sort of separated the civic portion of town from the more industrial section. The man had a very bright red and green fishing rod that Damon admired. "Nice rod you got there. Any luck?" the young man inquired. Fisherman responds, shaking his head and smirking. "Just felt like having catfish for dinner tonight. Think my timing is bad." Damon suggests, "Just say a short prayer, make it up if you want, and then think about what you have to do after fishing, all the time while leaving your line in. Then think about what needs doing tomorrow. No guarantee you catch anything. But it's less likely you'll be depressed if you don't. Fishing impatiently is like watching a pot till it boils. Relax. If you caught them here before, they're still here. Just leave the line under your arm and rest on this bridge wall. If you catch anything, you'll be happy and not depressed. If not, at least you won't be depressed."

They chatted for another minute or two about the weather and its effect on fishing before Damon took his leave. When he was almost a block away and turned to go into his place of employment, he thought he might have seen a red and green fishing rod vibrating almost in a vertical position. He smiled to himself.

Damon worked well for the next week or so, being timely with his work assignments, and gave a normal impression to all his colleagues. Since all was going smoothly at present, he thought it a good time to contact Linda, the one he took to lunch recently. He phoned her at work and was told she was absent that day to illness. He would call back the next day he thought.

On his way home that day, he passes the young girl's house and thought he saw her getting into a car with a tall young man. It bothers him somewhat, but he figures why not. He didn't own her. He didn't know if this was his true feeling or rationalization. Anyway, he'd soon catch up to her.

Next day, Damon phoned Linda at work during lunch and got her on the phone. She was happy to hear from him and mentioned there was a hockey trip planned to see the Philadelphia Flyers next week. The bus and ticket price were $50.00 per person and included a meal at the game. She asked if he'd like to take her quite excitedly. He quickly agreed, mentally figuring how he would buck up for the trip. They spoke briefly during his phone call and promised to meet a day prior to the trip. Damon was glad to have contacted her. She didn't look like she was high maintenance. She just liked hockey, he concluded. He wanted to ask about the tall stranger, but figured why should he? He got a date with Linda and that's all that mattered.

At home that evening, he was alone about an hour after dinner since his mother had a dental appointment. He was sitting on his bed and caught sight of the full-length mirror on the wall. He rose and stared at himself. He tried to think of any movie star he resembled. Nothing came to mind, as he thought. If he became one, he wouldn't want to resemble any of them. Then he did karate moves in the mirror. He did fairly well till he tripped on the rug.

He would be more careful next time. He started flexing a couple of muscles next in his reflection. He would soon go to a gym daily and look like those guys in magazines. He also would someday play pro baseball and be a role model for all, young and old.

How he would accomplish all this was by taking a leave of absence from work when he hit the lottery. He knew he'd hit it. Felt sure God wanted him to. Soon he collapsed on his bed and slept an uneasy sleep, dreaming of playing hundreds of lottery tickets. He dreamt of failed movie auditions, karate mishaps, tiny muscles, and errors in a baseball game. He awoke in a cold sweat around 3 A.M. He freshened up in the bathroom and promised himself he wouldn't let friends, family or employees catch him planning his life. And when he did strike it rich, he would help even more people than he usually does. He would be famous. But for now, he had to be low key. His close life associates didn't understand this. So, he couldn't let them observe him planning. To them, it was daydreaming, but Damon knew better.

On the day Damon was to meet Linda to plan their trip, he was walking to her house when he saw the neighborhood beggar a couple of blocks before her house. The poor man was in that spot always, weather permitting. The young man gave him pennies and nickels whenever he saw him; and they became somewhat friendly, considering their different circumstances. Damon always had a fine word and a joke for the man, but the beggar had more jokes for him, so it was a good deal. Damon asked him why he begs. He says he can't steal. He says why not work. The impoverished street person admits he can't read. The youngster suggests he visit the elderly barber down the street and ask to clean and sweep the hair for a few hours daily; he wouldn't pay much, but more than he's collecting on the street. He takes the advice. He gets $3.00 a day, plus dinner with the barber and free haircuts. The old barber likes cutting hair but says he's too old to clean up or anything else.

The beggar is cleaner, groomed, and has better jokes for Damon when they meet at the shop. Damon soon learns that the best jokes start in barber shops.

Chapter 5
The big date and helping the poor

Saturday arrived; Damon and Linda boarded their bus with twenty others and had a pleasant ride to the city, talking, joking, holding hands and gazing for longer periods into each other's eyes than any of their fellow passengers. When they finally arrived, crowds were walking into the Spectrum for this rare day hockey game, pushing all, including Damon and Linda, into each other as all of them neared the entrance gate. No one seems to mind, especially the young couple from bus #4308 from upstate PA.

The game was great. Flyers won, and the crowd cheered; some hugged, some kissed, some danced. Damon and Linda were one of the couples that did them all. Afterwards they enjoyed their included meal; they both chose the crab cake platter while they spoke of things they had in common, like biking, swimming, reading, charity and families; and things not so much in common, like religion, money, life, marriage, and death. Anyway, they were having a good time, and that's all that mattered now.

After dinner, bus #4308's driver counted twenty-two familiar heads seated and settled, put the vehicle in gear and headed for the PA-turnpike to deliver his human cargo. Fifteen minutes into the ride over, half the people were snoozing, the rest were leaning towards it and the two youngsters fell asleep in each other's arms knowing they'd be alone at their destination. Upon arriving at the terminal, they woke, gave each other a quick serious look and knew what their next step would be when they arrived at Linda's house, if they could hold themselves together until then. There would be a quiet explosion in the girl's living room, hopefully without ripping any clothes. Damon wondered if it would be lust, sex, or love sex. He hoped for the latter. All he ever had before were the other two. They never made the living room.

As it turned out, Damon's car was parked in a portion of the terminal parking lot where the floodlight was burned out. Not fully dark, but pretty much. Funny thing, when they approached the vehicle, neither of them attempted to sit in front. They simply gave another quick glance, kissed and crushed their bodies together and almost fell in the back seat, locked in a fired embrace from which neither could cease.

How they removed the clothing necessary to conclude this animal like passion that possessed them both, defies logic. At least one of them must have had three hands, or more. Damon wanted to kiss every square inch of body in his grasp, but that would have to occur another time. A volcano was about to erupt, and he was powerless to slow it down. Linda's kissing and sucking his neck didn't slow anything either. When his blazing short but thick steel hard organ finally entered her, he guessed it would be over for him in less than ten seconds. That was about five seconds too high. He let out sounds that were almost inhuman. Less than ten seconds later, the girl's passion scream drowned his cry out. They held their embrace another three or four minutes, released each other, and knew this was not just a date. For now, they planned not to plan anything. The moment was too precious for talk. He said to himself, "Another good day."

Next day Damon wanted badly to see his new girl, but he knew her mother was home, and if he visited the house, he felt sure her parent would sense the electricity sparking between them, so he thought better of it. Anyway, he had to do his charity work at the shelter today. He was on kitchen duty today, assisting the cook by peeling potatoes, sautéing onions, cleaning, or steaming vegetables and helping serve the roughly forty poor homeless that attended. Afterward, a priest, rabbi, or minister would speak to the attendees while staff and volunteers ate their meal of the same food served to the needy. Everyone felt good afterwards; the poor weren't hungry; the workers felt they gave themselves to a very necessary job.

Content with himself after directing the kitchen helpers to prepare the meal for 24 homeless men and women, Damon casually thought of having some fun when he arrived home. Maybe he'd pretend he was a hero saving someone from a fire or stopping a robbery by knocking the gun from a thief's hand. He might save someone drowning or be a strong man lifting a car off someone's leg. He'd think of something. While strolling and contemplating his next adventure, Damon noticed Jimmy C pulling up 1½ blocks away and speaking to a couple of street toughs. He exited his patrol car, spoke briefly and firmly with one of them, and they each shook hands. When he returned to his car, one of the ruffians threw something on his front seat saying something like, "Buy your kids an ice cream cone," which Damon clearly heard since he was at present only 15 Ft. from the 3 of them. "Whadaya say Damon," the officer called, smiling and giving a short wave.

He approached the policeman, shook hands, and asked how he and his family were doing. "Some good days, some bad," reported Jimmy. "Mostly good so far." He smiled. "How bout you, Damon, what you up to?" "Just finished helping feed the homeless at the South End Shelter, roast beef, mashed potatoes and succotash with pumpkin pie today. Fed 24, 2 cooks and 4 helpers. Someone made a mistake and changed the recipes to 45 people. Needless to say, some people had seconds. It all worked out though, since guys usually take seconds, and gals seldom do," laughed Damon to his cop pal. "How many did you have, Damon?" Joked Jimmy. "Can't waste good food, I always say," chuckled the young man. Still snickering, Jimmy asked where Damon was headed. "Home." Said the youngster. "Ever ride in a police car?" "Alright!" shouted Damon, climbing into the patrol car and patting Jimmy on the back. "Could you turn on the siren?" asked Damon, smiling at Jimmy. "Sure Damon," Jimmy said seriously, "But then I'd have to arrest you." Both men cracked up. Shortly Jimmy pulled up to his friend's house. Damon exited and asked when his next ball game was. "Day after tomorrow," answered the officer. "Take care, Damon." Damon watched him drive away. He swore he heard his siren for a few seconds. Damon saluted down the street, laughing while entering his home.

Chapter 6
The creek, Mike, and the truth

At home, all looked bright for Damon. He had a job, girl, charities, family and friends. He was happy. He was confident, maybe over-confident. He thought he'd look in the mirror, just for a minute and assume he was, "Oh, I don't know, maybe a movie star and a hero of some kind. Maybe I saved someone from drowning, or I'd be a star that did his own stunts. I'd always whip the bad guy, save the good folks, get the girl, be a role model and win hero awards, academy awards, stunt awards and civic awards with keys to the city. Why not go down to the creek now. The current can't be that bad."

Fifteen minutes later Damon was up to his knees in a steady flowing creek. He dove in with only shorts. It was pleasant for a minute. Then the slow current wasn't slow. He tried to angle himself back to shore, but to no avail. He pretended he was saving someone from drowning and would be a hero in the town. He felt important and tried to swim toward shore but kept getting pushed down stream and further from land. He paddled and stroked furiously but all he could manage was to stay afloat. Then he tried desperately to turn toward shore and swim as hard as possible in that direction with his head down. The young man pulled hard with both arms and kicked furiously toward shore, but all he accomplished was to wind up further downstream and from land.

The frenzied person knew he had to think fast. Somewhat further out Damon noticed a fair-sized branch growing out of the water. Fatigue was setting in fast because of his exertions, his fear, and the cool temperature of the creek in early autumn. He swam out to this farther limb partially with the current and upon reaching it hugged it hard, taking many deep breaths. He rested there for some minutes. He thought hard. First, he would check his present position and test the strength and firmness of the rooted branch he clung to for dear life. He pushed and pulled softly, then quite hard on the protuberance 'til he was satisfied it was a firm position where he could rest and gather much needed strength.

Damon hung on this growth for a while until the temperature caused more discomfort than the relaxation was worth. Wetting his head and face fully to be fully awake and aware, he looked around and saw another limb sticking above the surface but slightly further from shore. He dismissed this target until he noticed a second branch rather close to the first but closer to shore since land jutted out there. He swam hard to the first, again partially with the current and rested for a minute. Gathering strength and resolve, he headed hard for the next station, knowing he's now against the current. Knowing this fact he kept his head down except for brief breathes, and headed by dead reckoning to the closer branch to shore. If he overshot, Damon figured the outbound current would carry him to the desired spot. He did, and it did. Holding onto this closer respite, he saw one more branch closer to land than his present one. If he could regain this last one, he could possibly swim or wade ashore and be out of this mess he created for himself.

He pulled himself together, thought and prayed fast, threw water on his face and lunged toward this last location. When he thought he was all in, he looked up and saw the limb ahead of him roughly a yard and a half. He summoned his last bit of power, half swam, half-lunged and almost jumped from the creek to reach this pinnacle of life. He did so, but barely, and breathed hard for 5 solid minutes, holding onto the life-saving piece of wood. Following this he swam against a weaker current, then waded ashore, thanking God, the angels, the saints, and the devil.

Damon sat on the shore for a few minutes, then started home. Walking home he thought, "was over confidence a problem?" He didn't want to say yes, but if he said no, there's a problem. "Hard to admit things," he thought. He didn't want to spoil the fact that he just saved his life. He felt somewhat proud, but also somewhat stupid. Not wanting to admit anything, he'd put that answer off for another day. For now, he'd stick to the mirror.

What Damon was unaware of when he was exiting the creek, was that Mike Sampson was jogging around the water for his daily run. Mike was aware of the overconfidence sometimes displayed by his buddy from previous meetings and discussions with him. He knew not what this creek visit by his buddy signified, or if it had anything to do with anything. He simply was aware of his friend's tendencies, and of his own wet encounter with rough flowing water for no apparent reason. He'd see him soon enough, he reasoned.

Even though Damon took aspirin, got a hot shower, and drank his remedy of tea, whiskey, honey and lemon juice that evening following his poor impersonation of Tarzan, he still had some sniffles when he awoke the next morning for church. He attended a service but quickly returned home afterwards to get to bed and recuperate before the work week. That evening he felt somewhat better, not 100%, "He'd be ready for work though" he surmised. He had to. There were bills, there was money for his mother and especially for him and Linda. Then out of the clear blue sky he figured to himself, "What problem, I don't have any kind of confidence problem, over or otherwise. Just an active imagination. It's the others, with no imagination, that have the problem." He thought he believed this.

Next day Damon's mother was at her supervisor's job at the Goodwill Headquarters Center. When she left home, she couldn't find her key, so she left the front door unlocked since Damon was home because of his company doing repairs at his building. Mike visited him, found the door unlocked, came in and heard Damon talking and other noises from the upper floor.

He ascended the stairs, peeked in Damon's room and saw his friend flexing sparse muscles, talking into a fake microphone as a football star being interviewed, as a rock star singing, bumping and grinding, and as a hero that discovered a cure for cancer. Mike entered the simple bedroom and startled his buddy. Tells Damon he heard about him doing this stuff before, and he also confessed he witnessed a wild outdoor escapade a few nights ago. Mike didn't think it was serious before. He thinks it is now. Damon argues, "It makes me feel good and its fun." Mike retorts, "It's not fun pal, its nuts." His friend argues further, "I may be one of these people someday." "Damon!" shouts Mike. "You better quit thinking that way if you want me as a friend. This is for your own good. This has got to stop. By the way, how come you help people with advice and good examples, but not yourself?" quizzes Mike. "I do help myself," shot back Damon. "That's where the good days come from. I can only help myself Mike, not change myself." "Listen buddy," says Mike loudly "if you insist on this nonsense, you at least better stop believing it to be real or even possible." "But I could be one of these in the future," repeated Damon. "Damon, shut the hell up!" screamed Mike. "Stop talking like a nitwit. You can be one of these? Yeah, sure Damon. And the moon is cheese, the earth is flat, my aunt's my uncle, and the sun shines at midnight. Damon, you have everything. You have a job, girl, family, friends and health, even with that weak mind. Don't screw it up. Many would trade places with you. I love you as a friend, Damon, but this act has to go. Help yourself like you do to others." "I know, I know Mike," said Damon. "But we all know it's always easier to advise others than yourself. I'm just better with others." "Ok Damon, bottom line," continues Mike, "Change or lose a friend. I care for you, but I can't watch this nonsense," said Mike, slamming the door to Damon's room. Damon sat quietly on his bed, thinking, "is Mike, right?" He stands, looks in the mirror again, but his heart is not into fantasizing at the moment. Maybe tomorrow.

Chapter 7
A lawyer friend, Damon attacks the drug problem

Damon occasionally felt religious and when this feeling hit him, he'd go to confession with father O'Brien at St. Luke's. On one particular day, he overheard a man that sounded like a lawyer talking to another of the parish priests in a nearby pew. The lawyer was telling the priest various things that centered mostly on job problems because of scarcity of clients due to him being the new kid on the block and much competition. Damon exited the confession box, greeted the priest in the pew and was introduced to the new lawyer in town and they talk. Lawyers name is Frank Papal. Damon invites him to his house, they have coffee, and Damon shows him plaques in his room from various volunteering activities. Lawyer is told Damon may have a client for him that is seeking disability award because of a severe foot problem he has had for some time. Says he will visit Frank with a client. Lawyer asked "when"? Damon says he'll try to get client tomorrow early in the evening. Maybe around 5 P.M. suggests Damon, flashing five fingers at the lawyer.

As it turns out, Frank and the client appear three times before a judge, and on the third try, the man was granted an award of $66,200 of which Frank kept $22,066.

He thanks Damon; Damon suggests always treat them as you would want to be treated if you were in their shoes. Half the time this strategy actually helps retain clients. Lawyer gets more clients as word spreads.
Eventually lawyer hires small staff and desires larger office. Damon assists him with zoning permits and any local requirements for the office site thru his company and its engineering expertise. Frank occasionally assists Damon with parking tickets and advises him of finances, wills and legal matters relating to his job and his company where he worked. They sometimes visit, pal around with Mike, or just have a beer or two every week or so. Damon eventually tells Frank of his feelings for Linda Dijoseph and his plans in that direction, preliminary as they were. Frank is happy for him and wishes him luck.
He suggests Damon find out all he can about her, her likes, dislikes and what she expects of him. And by no means don't let her go, since she sounded great. Frank Papal was a smart man and a smart lawyer. As the time went on, he would eventually change courses and become an assistant D.A., then the D.A. of the city, common pleas judge, then a judge of the superior court of the state of Pa. But that was in the future. At this time the young lawyer was busy building his first practice and a new family.

Frank was engaged to a teacher, and they were expecting their first child in six months. They had agreed to conceive a child as soon as Frank passed the bar exam, and it took about three months for conception to finally occur. They thought children are first, wedding vows second. Both realized vows were only voices in the wind. If love existed, vows or no vows won't affect a person's situation. You either commit or you don't. Frank would sometimes joke, "you can't be half pregnant."

When Damon confessed to his legal friend his occasional daydreams, Frank advised him to keep that to a bare minimum. He said it's ok if it's very seldom. But if it interferes with life, love, family, jobs or friends, there's a big problem.

Damon related his buddy Mike's outlook on Damon's tendencies. Frank agreed and stated he would have been an echo in that room where Mike gave his very strong opinion. Damon promised himself he would start controlling his problem. Frank asked why he fantasized. Damon flatly said, "It makes me feel good," half lying. "It stops me from being depressed," would be a lot closer to the truth. Frank's logical follow up question was why don't you already feel good. Damon's answer stunned the young counselor. "Because of modest finances, old car and clothes, lack of a girlfriend prior to Linda, small room in a small house, not strong, brave or handsome, brainy or gifted with special ability. I'm only thankful for favoring my mother more than my father in looks. She was much better looking than him." Frank stared in disbelief. "Damon," he half shouted, "do you listen to yourself? A dangerous fault for people, especially young one's like you, is taking things for granted. What about home, family, job, girl, car, clothes you do have; friends, volunteering, and oh yeah, a little thing like health. Talk to me when you're starving, jobless, homeless, girl less, friendless, and very ill. Pal, don't fall into the trap of taking things for granted. Don't fret on not possessing. Thank God, nature or whatever for what you do have. You know what life owes you? Zilch. Nada. Seriously Damon, life owes you zero. The only thing perfect in this world, is imperfection. Think about this conversation pal. It's not me talking Damon. It's the real world. Deal with it. You won't be sorry."

A few weeks after Frank opened his new office, he recalled the help he received from Damon regarding the local ordinances he adhered to for the purpose of complying with the towns planning and zoning laws.
The lawyer about that time had made a detailed study of all state and local requirements governing new and existing commercial and industrial sites, and to a lesser extent those of residential properties. After spending six months off and on understanding local and state ordinances and standards relating to all imaginable property whenever time permitted, he made a request of his buddy. He simply wanted a chance to represent M.A. Clinton Inc. on any projects requiring adherence to local requirements, agreeing to charge a lesser lawyer fee than any competing law firm for the same work. Damon presented the proposal to executives at Clinton, and shortly after the firm gave a positive reply. Frank was quite thankful, inviting Damon, Linda, Mike, and his new wife and one of Frank's legal associates to dinner at the lawyer's home. The evening was pleasant and uneventful, save for Frank toasting Damon as a great and trustful new friend, after which they shook hands and gave a quick hug. When it was time to depart, Frank offered tasty leftovers to Damon since Frank's girl always made extra. Damon gratefully accepted knowing immediately these parcels of food would be left at the corner under the bridge where the homeless migrated. He did so before he drove Linda home, and both were

thanked by about five or six poor souls, Damon then took Linda home to an empty house, where it became a repeat of their backseat love making, except that they now were like human beings using a bed for their passion fires of love. When they were sated, they relaxed and studied the ceiling. After a brief interval, Linda interjected, "Damon, I know this is fast, but don't you think we should at least plan our future?" Damon knew this had to come pretty soon and it made him want her even more. But there were practical considerations. After a brief kiss he promised her to start planning.

But admitted it will take some time. She was satisfied for now. He actually wanted to marry her. He would figure out apartments, bills, jobs, and finances as soon as possible. And he also was willing to avoid full-length mirrors in any new dwelling place. Or maybe just hide one.

Speaking of mirrors, he checked his out as soon as he arrived home that evening. He couldn't resist and killed a ½ hour talking, posing, flexing, and conversing with imaginary characters. He would stop this soon he thought, but for now it made him feel good. He then had a great thought, listening to the news report on his bedroom T.V. stating drug abuse was on the rise in the region. He would help solve the problem. Tomorrow he would go to the distribution point of the neighborhood and start straightening out the poor addicts.

Chapter 8
A legal steal, intro to drugs and reality

But before he could plan his addict visit, he got an urgent call from Frank, his lawyer friend. It seemed Frank lent out his local zoning and other ordinance books to a client that was out of town. The lawyer was now working on a project for another client that was due the following morning. Without these books he couldn't complete the job. During the phone call, Frank related this, and requested Damon to lend him his company books just until he finished his project tomorrow, when he would return them. Damon agreed, and the lawyer headed to Damon's home. But while he drove to his friend's house, Damon realized his books were at his job location, since he wasn't taking home any work lately. When Frank arrived, Damon told him and they now had a problem, since Damon's job building was now locked for the evening. Damon thought for a minute.

He recalled how basement windows locked and knew it only took a thin blade to release the spring-loaded lock atop each window. He also remembered that the alarm wasn't wired to these windows since they were so narrow and usually had much mud and water next to them due to gutters emptying beside them. Also, various dogs and cats used the rear of the building at and around these windows to relieve themselves. Anyone trying to gain entrance to the building from there must be quite thin and be desperate to steal office papers of no value except to trained personnel, not to mention the necessity of laying in this mud-laden animal outhouse to enter any of the windows.

Damon asked, "When do you need these books?" "The sooner, the better," Frank exclaimed, "but I must have them by 9 P.M. the latest if I am to finish in the morning." Damon paced a minute in the small bedroom where they were talking. Frank asked, "What do you think, Damon? Can you get them by then?" Damon looked at his buddy, nodded and gave thumbs up, Frank asked, "By nine?" Frank saw Damon raise nine fingers. The lawyer let out a sigh of relief.

The young man quickly donned old work clothes and took the short drive to his company for a quick nocturnal visit. He had an old raincoat to lay in beside a window and a shovel and flashlight he kept in his car for emergencies, both of which he was sure to need. He also had a fishing knife in the glove compartment, which would do nicely to unlock a window. He drove directly to the building rear, which hid his car from the road, got out and unloaded the tools he had. He soon selected a window, laid his raincoat beside it after shoveling as much dirt, mud and debris downhill from the building as he could, and started feeding his knife between the window and frame until it hit what was a spring lock. He knew from being in the basement searching the company archives for old documents that all windows had the lock in the center of the window, so it was simple to judge its location after two or three tries. When his knife finally hit something that sounded metallic, he knew he hit a lock. Moving his knife sideways back and forth, he was able to whittle away enough wood from the frame to hit the edge of the spring-loaded bolt that held the window to the frame. He pushed down the knife point onto the bolt end less than ¼ of an inch, since he knew the bolts did not rest inside the hole any more than this. With flashlight in his mouth, one hand on the knife and the fingers on the other hand on the wooden side of the window, Damon pushed down the bolt with the knife and pulled the window toward him with fingers and fingernails. Once open, he saw a landing spot for himself with his flashlight and entered the basement feet first and landed on the table he knew was next to this particular window. With the flashlight guiding him, it was simple to climb to the main floor, locate the needed books, and place them in a thick envelope to protect them from any outdoor mud or debris beside his entrance and exit window. Damon stood on the table, placed his envelope of books outside the window on the raincoat, and pulled himself up to the window opening by pulling on the outside brickwork left and right of the window frame and jumping toward this opening to propel himself thru the small window opening. It took three jumps to shift enough of his weight from inside the building to the outside onto the raincoat. This accomplished, he rested a minute on the opening and raincoat to catch his breath, then stood up, gathered belongings and books, and replaced jimmied window in place, planning to relock it the next day he was at work, since no one ever checked such things.

He brushed himself off, disposed of the filthy raincoat in an outdoor trash can, placed his belongings in his car and drove to his home. He quickly showered, and while toweling himself phoned Frank to come and collect the much-needed books and booklets. It was 7:45 P.M. when the anxious lawyer entered Damon's room, where the young man's mother directed him. After thanking him profusely, Frank asked what time he needed them back in the morning. Damon, too tired to talk while finishing dressing, flashed eight fingers at Frank, who nodded in agreement and rushed out of the room. Damon laid back on his pillow and collapsed in clothes he never needed to put on.

Next day after work, and after repairing the window on his lunch hour, Damon goes to addict hangout to try advising them to quit their habits. Two are convinced to go home, at least for that day, but there are little positive results from his speeches, except for some curiosity regarding this nut on the corner telling people to stop the only thing they live for. Unfortunately, though, there was a negative effect. While Damon was relaxing after his talk by sitting on a milk crate on that corner, he observes two addicts sniffing coke and enjoying the effects of it. Damon is convinced to try a snort or two as a free introductory offer, just like the offers stores make. Does so. He enjoys it. Is given another freebie. Likes it more. Needs it more. Buys the next one for $20.00. Feels happy and relaxed, finds out when his new contact is on the street next. Damon says he'll see him then. Goes home and next day tells Mike how he tried curing addicts and failed but got free doses for himself. Both young men are outside Mike's house where they were headed for a beer after work when Mike hears this. He grabs Damon, shoves him inside his house, and slaps him hard in the face.

Mike quickly apologizes but exclaims to his friend "I did that cause I care, pal. And I don't want you addicted. But Jesus Christ, Damon, who the hell do you think you are, trying to solve a century's old problem by a pep talk. Do you realize how many people and dollars have been thrown at his deadly habit? How many sands are on the beach?" Mike continues even louder, "While you're at it, why not try to stop smoking, alcoholism, rapist and murders. Oh, yeah, and in your spare time you can try for world peace." Damon was quiet. Mike continued, "Buddy, this is the real world. You got free drugs to hook you. I guess it worked. Stop all this grandeur and fantasy and wake the hell up. Keep helping people. You have a knack for it. And it will help you keep out cravings and make believe from your troubled brain. Do it, before it's too late." "Damon," shouts Mike. "Can you stop this on your own?" "I don't know," comes a weak reply from his friend. "You're going to rehab then. I know you just started using, but this is one habit you can't try to break too early, only too late. I'll square it with your mom. She trusts me." "But what about my job, girl, family, friends, and my life?" cried Damon. "You're no good to all the above at this point in time. Should 'a thought of that before you went and partied with the powders."

Damon enters rehab. Has rough few days at first. Then gets slightly better on the fourth day. But is slow getting back to himself. Advises couple of addicts to quit while trying to do so himself. Never finds out if he helped them. Has his own problems and tries going to gym in the rehab center to occupy his mind? Exercise and sweat temporarily delay cravings and sometimes he sleeps following a gym shower and this delays tendencies a bit longer. But he can't sleep forever.

So, when not exercising he tries reading. Finds books have much fantasy, just what he doesn't need. Sticks mostly to history. Figures that's something that started at the beginning of time, and it never ends. Uses this routine for two weeks and when he is eligible for release, he applies for it. Is told release is possible, but he is allowed to remain a week longer and is advised to do so. He refuses and against better judgment of M.D. and psychiatrist is released on own recognizance. Helps couple people when he gets out and still has leave of absence from work and returns to addict hangout and gives speech of evils of addiction he learned in rehab. He is robbed and almost beat up by three hard-core addicts. He can scale fence before they catch up to him. Words echo in his brain, "This is the real world. Deal with it." Mike asks about marks on face. Admits robbery. Mike reminds him "Keep busy Damon so you can keep out foolish thoughts of grandeur and saving the world. Help those in shelters and on the street. Do what you do best." Takes advice for now.

Chapter 9
Stopping a thief, the truth hurts, where's the beef?

The day following his release from County Rehabilitation Center for Drug and Alcohol Abuse, Damon saw his friend the beggar heading to the barber shop where he worked. He asked how the forever street urchin was doing and was pleased to find out the man was happy and befriended the old barber. He certainly looked well with clean clothes, groomed, combed hair and clean shaved from the straight razor he received from his new employer. The grateful man inquired about Damon. He said he was doing well, knowing the poor man would just see thru the lie. While they conversed, the former beggar tells Damon about his friend the thief.

Damon then tells the thief of their common friend and advises him against crime and asks what he thinks jail is like. He's pretty close in his idea of prison, and Damon uses his knowledge to dissuade the robber from his present life. He asks why man steals. He says, "Cause people don't give ya things, and I didn't finish school cause my parents didn't be in it." Damon goes home, finds old books in the attic and next day gives them to the thief, suggesting he read them and go to a school that preps for G.E.Ds and then take the test.

He promises poor man if he receives G.E.D. he will bring him to plumber he knows that needs a helper. Thief laughs, takes books planning to sell them, but curiosity gets best of him, and he starts reading. The next few days he continues stealing to live but reads when he can. He goes to G.E.D. prep school, finds out requirements. Finds out he's been reading exact books required for G.E.D. test, requests taking test and does so passing and eager to meet Damon's plumber friend. He remembers Damon scribbled plumber's address in books he left with him, goes there, and mentions Damon's name and shows his G.E.D. Plumber is tired, needs helper and former thief begins his apprenticeship in plumbing. He works more and steals less; takes journeyman test and passes and soon after his only income is from plumbing. He thanks Damon in his thoughts.

Damon does fair for remaining leave of absence. Feels somewhat better during this shaky period during which drugs and fantasies slide in and out of his mind, with Damon trying his utmost to keep them out and not to see Linda for fear of provoking a painful scene. He recalled her words quite clearly, "It's me or drugs and fantasies." This was satisfactory to both for the present. They agreed Damon must phone daily, speak of his activity or lack of it, on a particular day, and he would always end the call with "I love you more today than yesterday, and less than tomorrow."

Damon also recalled his friend Mike's words. "Damon, do what you do best. Not drugs, make-believe worlds or any such nonsense. Help people. You're good, you enjoy it, and many need you. And just as important Damon, it occupies your mind. Fill your mind with people so you can keep all the bullshit out" was the gist of his friend's persuasions. He knew he was right. Both for that matter. He wondered how Mike and Linda would hit it off. They both made sense; they thought along the same lines. Damon couldn't think of a better match for her beside himself. No matter. She's always going to be his anyway, he figured.

During this period Damon met the high school student that lived next door to him. Often Damon heard the boy's mother hollering and beckoning the teenager to do homework. One day Damon saw Johnny Carr outside just walking back and forth, looking preoccupied and quite visibly upset. Damon excused himself and introduced himself as next-door neighbor and told of voices he often heard when windows were open. He tells the poor boy he's only trying to help, hopefully preventing the student from swinging at him. Damon wasn't afraid of him; he just had enough trouble on his plate and didn't need more. Damon confessed he surmised from the loud conversations that homework was the bone of contention. The student says he has no interest in school. Damon, request they sit on step while telling boy not to think of it as school. "Think of it as life. Math is money, buying, earning, winning, batting averages, height, weight, blood pressure, odds on how long you'll live and everyday things. History is what happened, what will probably happen again, why leaders don't learn from mistakes, and what good occurs when they do learn. English is how we talk to communicate thoughts in a clear and concise manner and how to convince and to lead. Social studies teaches to get along with others; where would we be if no one did? Sciences teach how things are made and not only teaches how to construct or understand objects but also how to repair things. Not just objects, people too. How can a doctor fix you up if he doesn't first of all know how you're made? They're all about life, not school. Many famous, important people started in school as the springboard for later life. Sports, movies, military leaders, rock stars, government leaders, hero's, inventors and mostly anybody. Just remember, its life. Add what you learn in school to what you see and learn on the street, from family, friends, working and playing. That's the whole picture. School is part of it. When Damon was quiet, the boy looked at him, started to say something and stopped. He asked Damon to wait a minute on the step as he entered the house. Damon agreed. Half a minute later the student reappeared with his geometry book asking about a specific problem in chapter three. Damon was lucky he knew the answer. He explained rest of chapter is based on that problem. Boy thanked him as he retreated back to his doorway still looking at the pages. Damon thought "Just maybe." During the days Damon heard no screaming from next door to his home when windows were open which was about ½ the time. Maybe he helped the boy, or maybe they spoke softer in nice weather. Damon bet on the former.

During this time Damon didn't display any fantasy like behavior in public or even to friends and family. He did occasionally go before the mirror in his room with the door locked and pretended one thing or another. He knew it was wrong, but he figured it's better than showing other people.

He kept speaking low when his role called for talking and for the most part kept a low profile. He refrained from drugs also during this period, but just barely. He had help from unexpected forces. Damon's mother always kept emergency money in the house for just that reason. Both he and she knew its hiding place. Additionally, Damon had his own secret cash stash, which was known only to him, so he thought. But whenever his mom left the house, she would take her emergency money with her, and unknowingly to Damon, his stash as well. She gambled he wouldn't check while she was out. She had to; she knew his tendencies. After one of these fantasy trips before his mirror one day, Damon had an unshakable urge to have a fix. He went to his stash and found zero, same with his mother's hiding spot. Since his mom was out, there was no source for drug money. But when he opened the fridge freezer, he found what he wanted. A bright red fresh frozen pot roast purchased yesterday and marked "extra lean premium beef pot roast double pack." It was two pot roasts packed together for $1.49/lb. Each roast was almost seven pounds. Both were worth $20.00. He figured that could buy a cheap fix some place. Damon left the house with his frozen meat and headed for the neighborhood drug hangout. The first pusher he met laughed at his proposition and walked away from him. There was one more young kid milling around and Damon knew he had seen him before. Damon asked what he could buy with $20.00 worth of beef. The kid saw the meat when Damon un-bagged it, put it back in the bag, and tried to run with the bag. Damon stopped him, kicking him in the shins, and the kid went down. Damon ran around the corner, and the kid tried to chase him, but stopped and thought, "How bad do I need this meat? If I try to sell it, I'll have as much success as this stupid bastard.

And any idiot trying to buy drugs with meat sure as shit don't have any real cash on him." So, the kid just watched as Damon disappeared down the street. Damon was just thankful he'd replaced his mom's roast before it was noticed to be missing.

The run slightly diminished Damon's cravings for the present and he tried to think of other things. He knew only one way to soothe his cravings for a fix. He would visit Annie the whore who was now a waitress. He rang the bell, lucky to find her home, and explained his situation. Annie thought quickly, either she gives him sex, or gives Damon money for drugs. Knowing sex won't hurt anybody and it's cheaper, and drugs wouldn't help anybody, she did the favor the only way she could. Damon begged her beforehand "Annie, try to get everything out of me. Maybe some of my yearnings for drugs will leave me as well." She did her best and when Damon was fully drained, he slept on her bed a very restful sleep. He awoke feeling much better, with his cravings still present but now he felt he could fight it. "Who says drugs reduce sex desire?" he thought, "Just phony news propaganda." He thanked Annie, she kissed his cheek and wished him luck and he went home, sneaking quietly back into his bed, falling asleep wondering who he would help next to occupy his troubled mind.

Chapter 10
Suicide, the nymph, and overdose almost

Next day Damon awoke to the T.V. news he heard downstairs. His mother raised the volume so she could hear it while she did her work. It happened that a man was atop the suspension portion of the bridge over the creek where people fished. It was a wide rather deep body of water to be referred to as a creek, but it was. The poor soul was threatening suicide supposedly because he lost his job and his wife left him and other troubles the broadcaster was announcing. Damon didn't know exactly what he could do but figured he should try. After all, he was told by Mike, that's what you do. When he arrived on the scene, police were all over it seemed, and one officer was speaking loudly into a megaphone like thing trying to change the man's mind. Damon knew this was wrong. Anybody knows the first thing to accomplish is to calm a suicidal person down. He said this to one of the policemen guarding the scene, and the cop recognized Damon as the local young man that helps the poor and troubled in the neighborhood. Damon waved at two more familiar officers from his area, and they gave a short salute to him. The captain in charge noticed this and inquired who this guy was. The officers told him while they conversed.

Damon got as close to the bridge as possible without going into taped off areas. He requested politely to try to dissuade this person from on high from splattering his organs all over the bridge, the steel structure supporting it, and the water beneath it. The officer figured he had nothing to lose, except the suicidal man, and he was losing him anyway if he didn't do something quick. The captain got Damon into position to speak in clear friendly tones to try and gain the poor man's trust and relax the poor soul. The man gave Damon the finger. He ignored it and continued speaking forcefully, but friendly. The man stared at him not uttering a sound. Damon started explaining how painful it was falling and hitting a hard surface when it isn't fatal; and that it usually isn't for a while; a long while it will seem. Also, how drowning in misery feels if the fall doesn't kill you. And how leg, arms and neck twist and break when hitting flat on water from great heights, and how you wish you didn't jump, due to fright as soon as you do." "It might be quick" he said, "But don't bet on it" Damon warned.

"It's not like movies," he laughed. The movies don't show someone vomiting and losing his bowel contents due to sheer terror while falling. The man on high hesitates and seems unable to decide what to do next. Damon is urged to keep talking to man and try to get him to speak to Damon. Damon asks his name and why he is on the bridge. Confused man explains losing job, financial problems, and problems with family because of shortage of cash. Man begins to cry and says he sees no other way out. While this is transpiring two policemen are sneaking up to man by climbing from the opposite bank of the creek. While Damon converses with man police creep behind him and clasp rescue harness that snaps around torso from behind the person and is a tight fit to anybody because of self-tightening feature. The other end of it is chained to bridge steel. The man struggled and fell the five feet the chain allowed and hung swinging. Fire department cherry picker later took man down and suicidal person was taken to county psychiatric hospital for counseling and arrested for trespassing. Damon was tired and left after being thanked for effort; he never saw man again.

On his way back home, Damon noticed the girl people called the nymph. If she was, Damon never had the pleasure. When he approached her, he asked if she was in the mood for anything. She said she always was. Then Damon thought better of it. He needed no more problems like a disease, so he said he can't cause he suddenly felt sick because of his encounter with the suicidal maniac. The girl heard about it and understood. Since he was with her, Damon tried to warn the girl how her ways could lead to HIV, Aids, gonorrhea, and any other painful disease if she didn't soon cut back on sexual activities with anyone she met, not matter who they were.

If not, he warned, at least use protection of some kind. She can't stop she claims but agrees to protecting herself. He felt a book in his pocket and pulled it out and saw it was a prayer book from church. He gave it to her, not really expecting her to read it, but it was worth a shot. She laughed at him but took it because she liked the leather cover on it. He told her to look at it when you have nothing to do. She starred at him, still rubbing her fingers along the leather cover. He said so long and good luck, started walking away, and after walking twenty feet turned around to see the girl leafing thru the pages, just out of curiosity it appeared. Damon said a quick prayer for her knowing she probably needed a miracle. The exhausted young man went home and straight to bed, no drugs, no mirror, no nothing.

He slept well except for a nightmare early next morning. He was falling off a bridge. Damon remained home all day until his monthly at his church. He phoned Linda, spoke a few minutes, was assured she was doing ok, and left for church. While he was in confession, he overheard some men in the pew discussing various problems; job, family, financial and social pressures, and the usual middle-age complaints. As he left the confession box, he was seen by four men in a nearby pew. He confessed he overheard their problems. And they recognized him as a church helper. He admitted he wasn't experienced enough to figure out their problems, but just suggested they each get together with their individual families and pray together daily, even if for a minute or so. He knew everyone does their own thing, but just to pull together, even for just a short time can help simply because it's together. It's like pulling a rope. A lot easier when all pull in one direction.

Pulling and praying together won't solve problems by themselves. Just makes it more possible to do so.

While walking home, Damon stopped by his drug N.A. group and said he was only staying a short while since he was tired. He asked to speak first since he couldn't stay long. He said, "I know we all have unique problems, and without going into each one, just remember help each other on good days, because there will be bad ones. Don't sweat small stuff; too thin, too fat, too ugly, too imperfect, too this and too that. Forget that stuff, help yourself and each other when you can. There's no instant fix. Do what you think is right. Not him or her. You. You might be able to fool others about what's right; you can't fool yourself. And I repeat, nothing is a quick fix. Repeated efforts are the key, maybe just once a month like we're meeting tonight. Continuous efforts toward each is the trick. That builds strong trusts and friendships. Ever see a tree grow? No you can't. But it is as you watch it. It's just slow, but steady. But when mature it's immovable. Try to push on an old sturdy oak tree."

Damon went home to his small room in the small street and crawled into bed, not knowing if he could sleep or not. He tried not to think of any cravings and pinched himself all over to steer his mind away from certain tendencies. He even hit himself over the head once with a hammer he kept in his room, because it felt good when he stopped. He kept thinking how good if felt, refusing to think of any cravings. He dozed off being tired from all this activity.

After succeeding with most of the souls he tried to assist, Damon felt good and had to celebrate with drugs. He knew mother's bill money was in its usual place at this time and helped himself to it while she was taking a shower. He soon located a connection on the drug corner and enjoyed a very potent fix. Because of his recent absence from drug action, he doubled the standard dose that he injected into his arm vein. Heroin wasn't his usual thing, but he had it before, and it was more than satisfactory. The usual coke guy was in trouble with the law and temporarily disappeared. Damon enjoyed the sensation for ten minutes in his car. Then drove with an extra dose he bought for later. Damon is stable for one day but keeps thinking about extra dose purchased before. Drinks whiskey to try to forget the extra dose. Not working, drinks more to try to reduce craving. Finished ½ quart. Falls asleep for few hours. Wakes and has strong craving. Rushes to fetch last dose and injects another double dose. Feels good after strong heart-pounding sensation. Enjoys feeling for ½ hour before falling asleep.

Wakes suddenly because of having trouble catching breath. Finally catches it after what seemed like an eternity but was much less than a minute. Happens again, and he catches it in about fifteen seconds. Tries to relax sitting up in bed. Prays silently, hardly moves. Stares at flower in wallpaper design and tries to be calm. Stays still for six minutes and then is aware of his condition. Has broken out in a cold sweat and is somewhat cold. Thinks quick shower may help. Don't want to be on feet too long, especially in bath, for fear of fainting. Undresses quickly, showers in five minutes, and towels off in another five minutes. Knows he needs a doctor. Too late for secrecy, feels slightly faint. Knows he can't drive. Calls family M.D. and asks if he can make an exception and make house call. Tells nurse on phone its house call or 911.

She quickly asks M.D., he advises Damon to relax, ask for symptoms and is told about drugs. Arrives at the house in fifteen minutes. Explains to mother at door who knew nothing of call. Both rush up to the bedroom of her son.

Damon is having trouble breathing. After a truthful interview with M.D. is told that anxiety over desire to marry, fantasies, embarrassment because of fantasies and being in rehab, and severe damage to whole pulmonary tract from drug inhaling and injecting causes breathing problems and irregular heartbeat. This is compounded by strong doses of street rich heroin designed to attract first-time users. This strongly contributes to fainting spells and is a serious toll on his blood pressure. M.D. also sees potential signs of unclean needles in Damon's forearm. He is given a relaxer to calm his heart and himself which will temporarily stabilize him, if it's not already too late. However, Dr. Saul strongly advises him to admit himself tomorrow to hospital, unless he would like to do so now. If now, Dr. offers to drive him to location. Dr. Saul feels now would be much safer. Damon declines, saying he will admit tomorrow.

Next morning, he awakens, feels somewhat better and, although cravings are present, they are markedly decreased by scare the young man experienced the preceding night. Prior to leaving for her job, mother begs Damon to admit himself to hospital. He refuses. They argue. She leaves for work in a huff. Her son does not admit himself.

Chapter 11
Overdose not almost

On the following day Damon eats more, sleeps a little better, and thinks about returning to work, but realizes he has more leave of absence time and thinks better of it and remains off.

Sarah Cittone notices her sons improved disposition at this time and hopes she can reason successfully with him regarding admission during his brief period of relative normalcy. Again, he refuses her demands. He goes out and helps a few more people by donating food and small sums of money and tries to keep busy at the nearby soup kitchen by doing some odd jobs. Soon his cravings return.

Returning to his house he sits by the window and feels very depressed from his addiction and convalescing at home when, luckily, Damon sees his old drug connection pass his house. The desperate soul runs out the door and half screams at the peddler, "Where you headed Bill?" "To the corner Dame," came a swift reply. "I'll be there shortly," returned Damon. "I need a fix bad," the young man admits to himself. He wonders if his mom took the house money with her when she left for work that morning. He recalled she was late and may have left it behind. Damon ran to her bedroom dresser and opened the drawers of folded pillowcases. He reached for the one nearest the middle of the pile. Pulling it out he felt a bulge in it and breathed a sigh of relief. He knew his mother's logic. Any thief in a hurry wouldn't look thru each pillowcase. Just a couple on top and maybe the bottom one and beneath the entire stack.

Not stopping to count the bills; the frenzied man shoved a stack of twenties in his pocket and ran out the door of the house. He walks as quickly as possible; trying not to draw attention to his mission and in two minutes arrives at the infamous corner. Seconds later he locates his connection. They exchange greetings and Damon truthfully admits he's in need of something. "I have heroin," the peddler states, "but it's not cut yet to street doses." "When will you cut it?" Damon interjects quickly. "Tonight, in my lab at home," smiles the drug salesman, knowing full well this customer isn't waiting a few hours. Looking him over, the hoodlum doubted he could hold out a couple minutes. "I'll take it as is." Damon instantly stated. "Just tell me how to cut it."

Damon thought he heard some amount of water, sugar, and some fancy chemical solution he pretended to know all about. "Got it," he fibbed. He accepted a tiny vial from the druggie and handed over fifteen twenties. Hurrying towards his house, he half heard the druggie shout "I had to charge you more because of the purity of the stuff." "No problem," Damon shouted back, hurrying to his rendezvous with ecstasy. Three minutes later Damon was in his kitchen pouring half the pure drug into an empty vial he kept for this purpose along with less than a teaspoon of water and about ½ teaspoon of sugar. He didn't have the chemical, so he substituted a teaspoon of whiskey instead. Shaking the vial to mix the concoction, he then inserted his used needle into the vial, withdrew its contents and injected this into the largest vein he could find in his forearm. Damon enjoyed almost five minutes of joy and gratification. The floating on air young man then celebrated his ecstasy and feelings of pleasure with a pint of whiskey he saves to aid his sleepless nights. This fully brought mind and body into ultimate relaxation and complete physical and mental satisfaction.

Soon after this melancholy nirvana, however, Damon Cittone broke out sweating, felt a chill, felt faint and became quite sick. Ten seconds elapsed that felt like ten hours to the deliriously ill addict. He then vomited profusely for a long minute and almost fainted. He then sat on a chair, trying to relax. A minute passed and then Damon felt a pounding in his chest and dizziness began. Not having a clue, he tried to be calm. He drank a half glass of orange juice after stumbling to the fridge and sat down again. His symptoms were easing a little but were still pronounced. He sat, calmed himself, and prayed.

After three minutes, Damon's symptoms were less severe. He drank a little water and realized if he relapsed into his former state, he was lost regarding his next step. Cautiously he crept close to the chair by the phone and sat down. Ten minutes later he was snoozing in the same chair when a knock on the door awoke the drugged young man from a rather sound sleep. Damon slowly arose from his imperfect slumber and finds Jimmy Cal on his doorstep with a very concerned look on his face. He admits the officer in his uniform and asks wearily, "What's up?" Damon is told they have to talk. "You look bad, Damon," Jimmy utters. "So do you," returns Damon. "But for very different reasons, I'm sure." "Bet on that pal," smiled Jimmy. "I'll make it short Dame, since you don't look

like you can handle anything drawn out," snapped the lawman. "Go ahead Jimmy," said Damon intently. Jimmy, very intently started, "My son needs the operation we all dreaded, and needs it very shortly. When I enrolled the family in our health plan, I neglected to mention little Jimmy's pre-existing condition since that would have raised my premium substantially above my means. And I was betting the doctors were correct in their assessment that an operation may never become necessary since his tumor may never become malignant. They were not. I have enough now to pay the difference in my coverage, and for the operation itself. But I'm accused of stealing from drug pushers. I guess I need a lawyer. I think you mentioned one time you know one. Don't you?"
Concentrating on the problem of his friend seemed to lessen Damon's symptoms for the time being. However, the poor addicted soul still had to force himself to see thru his own malady and think as clearly as his poisoned mental state would permit to assist his buddy in his time of need. Damon stared at Jimmy asking, "You want a lawyer, you say?" The policeman nodded. "I only know one, and he's not the kind you need," returned Damon. Continuing, the partially dazed young man said, "I'm sure he can recommend someone reliable for you, but let's not get ahead of ourselves. Did you do it?" "Damon" hissed the cop loudly, "I said I have the operation money. I'm not gonna draw you a picture." Damon looked long and hard at Jimmy Cal. He could see by his friend's expression that he will do almost anything to avoid a scandal and then prison. Damon's heart went out to him. "Well," half-screamed the policeman, impatient to hear any feasible solution to his life-altering almost futile situation. "I'm

thinking Jimmy, please. You know I have troubles too." "What are they?" Jimmy C queried. "Maybe in the next life, Jimmy. Not now. Be quiet for a minute and let me concentrate." After a decent interval Damon recalled Jimmies reaction to his appearance when he first entered the house. "How did you say I looked when you first arrived here, Jim?" "Not good pal, not at all," admitted the police officer. Damon then forcefully stated to him, "you're a policeman J.C., you see people in all conditions?" "Absolutely," said Jimmy. Damon cut off Jimmy Cal when it appeared he would elaborate, asking him seriously, "How does someone look who's near the end of the line? Either from crime, drugs, or just not taking care of themselves?" "You don't mean you have a habit do you Dame?" Smiling at his friend Damon returned, "Now I guess you want me to draw you a picture."

There was a long five-second silence. Jimmy broke it. "In answer to your question regarding your appearance Damon," he said with glassy eyes, "a lot like you Dame, an awful lot." "You got that right, pal. Couldn't be more so," said Damon seriously, nodding his head. Looking hard into Jimmies eyes, Damon stated evenly, "Now listen J.C., if I help you out of this mess, will you do something for me?" "Anything," Jimmy quickly retorted. "Ok Jim, I'll take the hit for this crime if you do what I say afterwards, ok pal?" continued Damon. "Think hard now Jimmy Cal. How can you switch suspicion from yourself to me, for this business? You're a cop. Think like one. Right or not, little Jimmy's at the end of his line if daddy's in prison. That makes the Damon way the right way. Think, James Calahan, think. How we gonna pull it off. Think," Damon loudly whispered.

A minute passed. "You have a gun in the house Dame?" "My mom keeps one in her bedroom." Jimmy quickly ordered, "Get it, keep the safety on, make sure your prints are on it and pocket it. Now listen close. We're going to the drug corner. I'm arresting you for possession there. I'll get you some. While there, I will "convince" these salesmen that you robbed their stash, used the money for drugs, prostitutes, and gambling, and some risky investments. They will also admit that your thievery spanned 2 or 3 months. Little cash remains is what you'll admit. Don't worry about amounts. Drug dealers don't employ accountants. Well into 5 figures is close enough. During interrogation, for possession, you will confess to the robbery with a signed statement. Many in the precinct will witness your arrest and questioning. I will take you to a cell, lock it and leave.

You will beg me to return you home to get your medications for your illness. I will take you in cuffs to my patrol car to your house. You will get what you need, return the gun to its spot and return to jail.

Damon agreed. He then quickly interjected, "Jimmy, here's what you're doing for me. Keep an eye on Linda DiJoseph and my mom and anyone close to them. Help them, protect them, whatever they need in a time of trouble, give it to them. This may never happen, but if it does, be there. If you're wondering how you'll know what's up with them, I say you will cause you're you. A good person, a good friend and a good cop. Do it and I'll go in peace." "But Damon," started Jimmy, "you'll be better in a few days and..." "Bull shit!" cried Damon. "Do what I say ok Jim?" said Damon, evenly holding Jimmy's stare. "You got it pal," said Jimmy C., slightly glassy eyed.

They looked hard at each other. Jimmy hugged Damon hard. Damon's eyes wet Jimmy's shoulder.

All occurred as planned except the return to jail. Damon had a fainting spell upon arriving home. Jimmy or Damon's mother couldn't revive him. Only 911 emergency could, but hardly. "How's it look?" Jimmy asked one emergency tech. "You don't need to be a doctor to know he's in his last hours, or hour." Jimmy has to decide. Staying here raises questions officially and with Damon's loved ones. Leaving Damon to his loved ones is the decent thing to do. He would have to convince HQ that the moneys taken, and drugs injected were so vast that the man has little time. Jimmy left, got in his patrol car, went and halted. For now, he thought it just might be safer to wait ½ hour or so.

Meanwhile, EMTS leave. Damon refuses hospital, knowing that won't help.

Sleeps on and off for 10 minutes and finally lifts the phone. Calls Mike and Frank. Asks them to visit. Phones Linda. Tells her to come soon as possible. Detecting urgency in Damon's voice, she does so. He is nauseous and dizzy. Soon Linda arrives. Damon says he feels sick. He seriously professes love for her thru his dizziness and almost blacks out in his own bed. He demands she have a happy life no matter what happens. She interrupts, "don't talk like that, Damon, you scare me." "Don't be scared, please Linda, that's not what I want," "But," she interrupts. Damon covers her mouth with his hand. "Just listen," he begs. "Please take care of yourself. Make every day count. Enjoy yourself. Think of me. I'll always think of you. I've never been happier than when I'm with you. I'm tired now and going to sleep. Come back tomorrow."

He dozed of. She kissed him on the forehead. She turned to leave but changed her mind. Something told her to stay. He slept for an hour, most of it with Linda holding his hand to her face or to her heart.

Word somehow spread thru the neighborhood of his deteriorating condition, and people he assisted over the years arrived in his cozy little bedroom. Damon slowly awoke, and they talked of better days, joked to cheer Damon up and still others started arriving. The first dozen friends that visited Damon enjoyed his company one more time. But most of those he assisted in the past were not yet aware of his condition. The rest were just too late. Linda was the first to be aware of this, as evidenced by soaked tears on a slowly cooling hand.

Outside, while sitting in his patrol car, Jimmy Cal noticed a group of sad-looking people leaving Damon's house in tears.
He approached one of them, asking what happened. He got the answer he expected. He grieved to himself for a minute, then returned to real life. Now he must return to his HQ and sell his story. He had to.

Later, while searching thru Damon's personal items and papers, with Damon's mom's permission, Mike, Damon's buddy, found a sort of diary, but it said nothing of Damon. In it Damon listed by name all those he ever assisted in any way, progress they made, what else needed to be done for them, and an OK next to those who were completely successful. Over ¾ were OK'd. The diary had from 1 to 10 names on each page. 25 pages were filled out. The last 2 pages had 12 names at various stages of completion. On top of the front page of the book was written, "God help me, so I can help them."

Chapter 12
Blame and how not to be a cop

Jimmy Cal knew his time had come for him to protect himself as much as possible from allegations that were floating around the universe, even if only in rumor form. He had to find out what he could regarding the rumor's origin, the basic premise of its content, and most important, how he could dodge any accusations stemming from such statements. Jimmy was now glad he "convinced" the drug people in the area, that Damon was the one guilty of the alleged criminal activity. The dealers were more than happy to accuse the late Damon Cittone of any crime suggested by Jimmy Cal when being informed by the policemen what would occur if they didn't. The druggies were told in no uncertain terms that if they did not cooperate, a narcotics crime force would be formed to erase drug activity throughout the entire city.

And word would then be spread that the force was formed because of excessive open drug activity in Jmmy Cal's area and that all concerned were forewarned and disregarded said warnings. It's easy to imagine what the other 200 or so less obvious drug salesmen throughout the city felt toward those peddlers that disregarded said warnings and brought down such a reign of terror that cut off hundreds of thousands in income too many criminal types. Not to mention jail time, fines, and life changing conditions.

What would these uncooperative drug peddler' lives be worth on the street after word was leaked to the media and the other areas that their blatant activity caused such misery. Not a plug nickel. Not only did druggies in Jimmy's area blame Damon for the crimes, they convinced each other that they must get law-enforcement to be fully convinced of the fact.

However, if H.Q. claims Damon confessed to crimes since he knew he was going to die anyway, H.Q. could claim he lied to save his friend since he knew death was imminent and had nothing to lose. Jimmy could then counter with the statement that Damon would never admit guilt in a crime he didn't commit just prior to his death since this would cloud his memory with family, friends, and the community after his demise. He would tell the truth to save his friend from false imprisonment, knowing his survivors would greatly respect his "truth" to save a dear friend from a false accusation. Damon would feel his survivors would be disgraced if led to believe Damon committed a crime but allowed J.C. to be sentenced for the deed.

Jimmy C suspected how his accusation began. Officer Joe Monte wanted to rise quickly through the ranks of their precinct. His record was O.K., but not nearly as good as Jimmy C's. Jimmy's arrest and conviction record was quite higher, and his record for deterring criminal activity thru mentoring, guidance and sometimes, even fear, greatly trumped many policemen, including Joseph Monte. Simply stated, Monte was jealous of J.C. and his record at H.Q. So, when he saw a possible opening for an accusation because of Jimmy's regular presence at drug hangouts, he felt this was an opportune time to start a rumor of collaboration on Jimmy's part with known criminal types. Monte forced himself to reject the possibility that J.C. may actually be on official police business at these times. This premise was unsuitable for his purpose. The end result he aimed for was double-edged. If he could bring about an I.A. investigation of J.C., he might greatly enhance his own record by exposing a dirty cop, and simultaneously besmirching that of his greatest competitor with an indelible stain that could all but erase a brilliant career. This might be just the sort of push required to speed an ambitious officers rise thru the ranks, thought Joseph Monte.

Jimmy C had strong circumstantial evidence to support his suspicions regarding Monte's activities. On two occasions J.C. noticed Joe Monte's police cruiser slowly rolling by a known drug corner while Jimmy was on police business there. Jimmy noticed the officer stopping momentarily, checking his watch, quickly writing in a notebook, and then driving off. On these exact days when returning to his precinct, Jimmy felt a few strange looks from his fellow men in blues.

This, he reasoned, is not a coincidence. Soon after these occurrences, his captain advised him to remain away from said corner for two days and assigned him to a reconnaissance job a few minutes away from the location. When J.C. asked why the switch, he was told that the usual person handling the job was ill, and since the area was part of an ongoing investigation, a continuous surveillance had to be maintained. Jimmy reported to said spot for two days, reported comings and goings of suspects he was told to look for, and then returned to his normal routine.

But the strange thing was, when inquiring among officers at the other precinct, no one knew of any officers that were absent for health issues, Jimmy knew cops. If anything, out of the ordinary went on, cops knew about it. J.C. was once asked if he changed his barber. He didn't. Just cut the sides a little shorter, that's all. But a fellow policeman noticed it. And that was from across the street, with his hat on. If someone didn't report because of illness, cops would likely know his prescription, doses, doctor and diet. No one was missing from the other precinct. His captain just wanted Jimmy C. away from his usual corners; possibly until things cool off. Or until a certain rumor just runs its course. They knew, as did all police personnel, police administration does not want reports of possible misconduct in the ranks, real or imagined. And they will do almost anything to handle the matter quickly and privately, even if only a rumor exists. It's a known fact that anything unsavory that travels up the chain of command, will come back down much worse, much quicker and more often. The police Dept, Jimmy knew, is just another institution where shit rolls downhill.

But the fact remained that there was a possible inquiry into his activities on the horizon, and Jimmy C. had to deal with it. And a logical starting point would be with the source of the problem. Whenever Jimmy had some extra time, he attempted to shadow Mr. Monte on or off duty. His first few drives behind the officer proved fruitless since nothing unusual happened. But on three later occasions, office Monte was observed entering a residence two doors from the home of Annie the Matre 'De, formerly, Annie the sex expert. When Jimmy had his next coffee and donut break at the town diner, he quizzed

Annie after tipping her properly regarding the house two doors from hers.

Annie, suspecting Jimmy had an idea of the identity of those dwelling there, figured she'd come clean about anything she knew. Jimmy learned that two female inhabitants at said address were presently performing activities that Annie previously engaged in before her restaurant career. Upon hearing this info, Jimmy recalled that on the one occasion he remained parked close by the residence into which Monte entered in his personal auto, he observed the officer leaving the house three minutes after entering with a rather unbuttoned and disheveled uniform and quite red-faced. Not to mention the officer's quick looks in both directions upon leaving the house and his extreme haste in doing so. If all was normal at the present time, Jimmy would likely try to protect Monte from any accusations of impropriety. Or he may just try to forget about it. But times were anything but normal. For now, Jimmy C would simply retain what he saw. Another basic fact popped into his brain; cops know cops. If Jimmy C. knows Joe Monte's extracurricular activities, who else does? He figured he'd better listen more closely in the police locker room.

Nearly a week later, probably since the rumor still persisted, I.A. decided police administration to proceed as usual upon the investigation of the late Damon Cittone and/or James Callahan on charges of receiving stolen goods, weapons charges, robbery and attempted assault. Two I.A. detectives were assigned to the case. After questioning family and friends, all claimed Damon was a good young man that just fell into a terrible habit. No one could completely confirm or deny his involvement in the above crimes. All that all could agree on was his terrible addiction and occasional fantasies. A warrant was obtained for the accused man's premises, auto, and belongings. What was uncovered during these searches was some drugs common to most hangouts in the area, a gun registered to Sarah Cittone with Damon's fingerprints on the handle, and a few hundred-dollar bills with a fair amount of heroin residue within their fibers. Upon questioning nearby dealers to Damon's home, they all accused Damon of the above crimes. Funny thing though, they were almost adamant that their interrogators believe them when they accused the deceased Damon of the crimes. One of the investigators thought this to be odd, but it just reinforced the case against Mr. Cittone in the eyes of the other one. These facts, along with testimony of a few drug addicts noticing Damon speaking with known dealers on the streets summed up the case pretty much against the accused. Both detectives knew it was a somewhat strong case; in some respects, it was circumstantial though.

The only other avenues that could shed any light on the case was an interrogation of the surgeon that removed the tumor from Jimmy Cal's son's head, thereby saving his life.

But the two detectives assigned to the case, Bobby Simone and Danny McShane, were well aware of doctor-patient confidentiality privileges that existed in most states. However, they figured what did they have to lose by just talking to the medical man.

Doctor Louis Kahn was not in surgery but only had office hours on the day Bobby and Danny selected for a possible interview with the M.D. Upon entering his office, the two were advised that one more appointment followed the one now being handled, and that Dr. Kahn would be free for a few minutes prior to a lunch break. A half-hour elapsed when the two were admitted to the specialist's office and were then seated in front of the doctor's desk. The surgeon was a friendly type, asking if either man needed a drink or coffee before detective Simone stated the reason for their visit. Briefly, the policeman questioned, "Since there is a slight possibility of impropriety on the part of James Callahan and his possible possession of large amounts of cash, the police department would like to know an approximate amount Mr. Callahan paid for an obviously costly operation on his 3-year-old son Jimmy Jr.," Mr. Simone asked, with raised eyebrows. The M.D., sitting and facing the two with a slight smile returned, "I'm sure you're aware of M.D.-patient confidence situations that are granted throughout the land, in this case M.D. patient parent privilege since the patient is a minor. Do you know I can't even say if I ever even saw the person in question, let alone give a price for service? The only fact I can admit to is one that's already known in the community. I have done pro-bono work in the past for special cases and will probably do so in the future. Outside of that, my hands are tied. I hope I helped you somewhat, but I must have a quick lunch shortly and get some rest. The next two days will be packed with surgeries.

Thank you for visiting, and if I can ever assist either of you medically, don't hesitate to call." They shook hands with each other, and the two law-enforcers exited the office, receiving almost exactly what they expected prior to their visit. The two cops decided they had better have a little lunch themselves. They had some thinking to do.

"But what else do we have," reflected detective Bobby Simone half to himself and half to his partner Danny McShane. "Sure, looks like the kid pulled these heists according to what we have." The two were having a light lunch at a local burger eatery while they attempted to sum up what they had regarding the case against the deceased. "Yeah, it's kinda strong Bobby, it really is, but so circumstantial," added Danny, "Then why would drug dealers insist Damon was the culprit? What do they gain by blaming Damon?" added Bobby. "Look at it another way Bob," started Dan. "What do they gain by not blaming Jimmy Cal?" "I heard rumors too, Danny Boy. I also heard that they may have started with Joe Monte. But don't get me started with him. Did I ever tell you the time me and my former partner called for backup, and Monte was one of the backups? Well, he came with two other uniforms. They all exit their cruiser; guns drawn and start walking to our position. Gunshots start coming at us from our front. Two uniforms take cover, then slowly proceed towards us. But Joe Monte does not. He proceeds alright. Backwards. Straight to his unit. He gave new meaning to the word back up. Cause that's exactly what he did." "Ok Bobby, I've heard things about the guy also," said Dan. "I never worked with him, but from what I hear, I'm lucky I didn't."

"Wait a minute Dan," started Bobby, "While we're on Jimmy Cal, lets pursue that thought. If we accuse Jimmy, what about the evidence we found against Damon, circumstantial as it is? Do we throw it out? And one more point. Do we have as much evidence against Jimmy C., circumstantial or otherwise? What we have Dan, is Joe Monte, that's it. A lawyer would have a field day with Mr. Monte on the stand." "I understand that and agree Bob," returned Dan, "but what if we're wrong?" "You mean accusing Damon?" questioned Bobby. "Yes, about that," returned Dan. "Glad you brought that up, partner," replied Bobby. "Let's pursue that. If we're wrong, then a policeman just got away with robbing drug peddlers that ruin countless young lives with their poison and promises to young girls of acting and modeling careers if they sell themselves to get to the top in their chosen profession and to support their unbearable habit. And said policeman spent the loot to save his three-year-old son's life that is threatened with a brain tumor and actually does so paying for the surgery with his ill-gotten gains. This same policeman has and still mentors youngsters of all races, sexes or religions about avoiding criminal activity, and leads them in a direction that will most favorably influence the rest of their lives. That, Danny Boy, is what will happen if we're wrong." Bobby, fully sweating and almost crying added, "And Jimmy's being accused by Joe Monte? Who the hell is that?" Bobby wiped his face and eyes with a napkin and said to his partner, "Think about that while I hit the men's room." A few minutes later Bobby returned, left a tip on the counter and asked Dan, "Ready to go?" "Looks like I'm as ready as I'll ever be," said Dan. "You know, I hear Damon Cittone was a real ace in the neighborhood. Helped many people. A shame he had to stoop to crime to support his habit. But he did.

I'm sure of it. Who else could it be?" concluded Danny McShane. "Exactly," agreed Bobby, placing his arm on Danny's shoulder. "Who else?"

Next day during the shift starting announcements of the first precinct, the sergeant concluded with stating that there will be no internal affairs investigation of any personnel in said precinct. And any rumors to the contrary must be reported immediately to an immediate supervisor. Failure to do so would bring severe consequences to all responsible.

That evening a uniformed policeman was noticed in church by an altar boy charged with mopping the floor for next day's service. The boy noticed the cop praying, very hard it seemed, and with a slightly wet face. He prayed quietly for five minutes. Then quite clearly stated he was thankful for something. He concluded with the words "And I will always protect those named by him, even with my life, amen." The policeman rose, kneeled, made the sign of the cross and walked out of the church. The cleaner noticed the cop left something near his seat in the pew. The boy retrieved the nametag and ran out after the officer. "Officer Callahan," he shouted, "you forgot this." The policeman thanked him, and the boy was surprised at the officer's face. He was red-faced, and his eyes were tearing. But he wasn't sad. Not at all.

Chapter 13
A viewing and some street friends

When Sarah Cittone lost her husband to cancer many years ago, she was left with a quaint little 2-story totaling about 1250 sq. ft. in area with 3 small bedrooms, 1 ½ baths, and a living room, dining room, and kitchen all in one area. The one thing in her favor was that the property was 2/3 paid off since she and her late spouse owned it for almost all the 14 years their son Damon and the elder Cittone were both alive. And since they doubled mortgage payments when they could, which was often, they were each used to being frugal with their funds, which would now become a necessity since only one of them now survived. Higher equity in their home was their guard against catastrophe such as a job loss, illness or the one that had just occurred. Borrowing on the higher equity was one way to endure financial problems that must be-fall those that experience such catastrophes. The equity in the home was one way Mrs. Cittone and her only child, Damon, could thrive the past ten years without Damon's father, Robert Cittone.

The late Mr. Cittone's best friend was Louis Carton, the undertaker and director of "Carton Funeral Home". He and Damon's father bowled together on a team and attended social functions regularly when Mr. Cittone was well enough to do so. So, it was natural for Mr.

Cittone's burial to be handled by Carton back then, and just as natural for Cartons' funeral home to take care of the burial of the son of Sarah and Robert Cittone that cloudy day ten years after the burial of the boy's dad. Although the funeral was delayed more than a week because of exhaustive autopsies stemming from the police investigation of the robbery and Damon's subsequent death, the young man's death was announced in local papers and date of the viewing or wake was stated along with the name and location of the funeral home. Mass at St. Luke's Catholic Church and internment at St. John the Baptist cemetery were to follow the next day.

At the viewing were many relatives, friends, and acquaintances of Damon Cittone's parents and of Damon himself. Seated in the front row of seats were Mrs. Cittone with Frank, Damon's lawyer friend, Mike Sampson, Damon's close friend, along with Linda De Joseph, Damon's girlfriend.

Behind them were Damon's aunts, uncles, numerous cousins and about a dozen employees from M.A. Clinton Inc., where Damon was employed. Damon's boss was among those attending, and he spoke of Damon's value to the company to Mrs. Cittone and Frank. Father O'Brien was also present, since he would say the rosary for the mourners, and also would say funeral Mass the following day. He spoke well of Damon to his mom, Frank, friends, and relatives. There was a steady stream of visitors for about an hour at the start of the service, with inevitable tears being shed and condolences bestowed. While all was relatively quiet after most people had arrived, there was some kind of commotion in the rear of the funeral parlor near the entrance. When the priest and Mike went to investigate the reason for the noise, they were told by one of Cartons' assistants that a group of neighborhood street people were trying to gain entrance to the building, and the assistant refused them admittance. When Father O'Brien and Mike went outside, they saw a gathering a few feet from the funeral parlor's entrance. As soon as the priest laid eyes on them, he instantly understood. These had to be some of those that were helped by Damon over the years; especially when he was having rough times prior to his demise. The priest and Mike explained as much to the funeral home employee, and all were admitted and shown to the front row of mourners, where Damon's mom and Frank sat along with Mike and Linda. They formed a single file, and each was eager to relate their experience with Damon Cittone to those in the front row. And also, to the many that also listened some rows back, due to naturally loud voices of those that are accustomed to hard living. Each wanted to relay his or her story first, and they were quite loud considering where they were. They were all gently hushed by the priest and told they would each get a chance to speak to Damon's closest family and friends regarding their remarkable encounters with the deceased.

Soon after, when the funeral parlor once again became relatively orderly, there appeared a single file line of street-dressed mourners astride the front row of the survivors of Damon Cittone. There was: the beggar, the boy from the bus, the fisherman, the prostitute, the addict, the thief, the boy next door, the suicidal man, the nymph, two from Damon's drug group, a half-dozen homeless souls, one of the men from the church pew, and finally Frank, the lawyer. Frank had stories too.

The beggar told how Damon introduced him to the old barber and got him a job sweeping up, and how he now worked his way up to be an assistant barber. He also mentioned how thankful the aged haircutter was to have much needed help in his shop. Even sweeping was becoming strenuous for the elderly groomer.

Next was the boy Damon met on the bus that had no one to play with. He was thankful for Damon's advice on how to get and keep friends, and he now had so many friends that he showed off his pictures of his birthday party with almost a dozen young boys and girls around a birthday cake.

The fisherman followed in line telling how he learned patience from the young man, and how it paid off when he had a line in the water. Admittedly he didn't always catch a prize, but his catch did increase, and he even showed off a picture of him and a large freshwater trout he caught in a local tournament where he placed second in the finals.

Following him was the former prostitute Annie, who now showed off her new resume that was begun by Damon, and she told of how she became a waitress through this, and presently worked her way up to being a Matre' De at a leading eating establishment. She obviously omitted her past business dealings with Damon and many other males in the area, and simply stated that she was formerly an unemployed domestic. Damon actually used this pretext on her resume, reasoning that an employer would believe domestic work was more strenuous than waiting tables. A pleasant appearance was the only other helpful quality a waitress should have. That was never a problem for Annie.

Frank the lawyer also felt this was the proper time to relate how he was assisted by Damon in his career, and how the young man was mature beyond his years.

One of the addicts Damon spoke with also attended. He related how Damon made him have the desire to quit, and although he did not just yet, he at least was scheduled to attend rehab, which was always a first step.

The thief was next, and he was proud to be going straight at this time and told of how he was helped to be a plumber, and how he finished his apprenticeship and was now a journeyman.

The boy next door was familiar to Mrs. Cittone, and he let her know how he now viewed school from speaking with Damon and was proud to show a B+ report card.

The almost suicide victim was proud to show himself, and he admitted he was saved by Damon by his shouts at a bridge that almost fateful day. And he now told the mourners that he and his wife are attending counseling at the hospital and also with Father O'Brien, whom they both greeted upon entering.

The nymph did not admit her tendencies to people, but just simply stated she had a disease at one time from dirty living habits, and Damon taught her perils of letting any disease persist, and how to live and avoid such perils, by prayer and otherwise clean living and how she accomplished this. She also showed a recent medical report stating any traces of disease were negative.

The four men Damon overheard in church admitted to the front row that Damon's idea of pulling together may not guarantee positive results, but it is truly a necessary first step.

Two from the drug group practiced what Damon taught about helping each other on good days, because all days were not. This practice brought two friends together that would otherwise have not met.

The homeless were the final ones in line, and they told how Damon suggested they visit diners and restaurants in the area and ask for leftovers instead of searching garbage. Damon suggested they offer to sweep and clean up to deserve these unwanted foods. They did and were rewarded accordingly.

Once again Frank Papal spoke out. He related how Damon assisted him greatly. He told of jobs he got thru him, the borrowed books, and his precious friendship.

When the line of all visitors paying their respects was no more, Father said the rosary; there were last minute condolences and goodbyes, and people drifted out. Tears were still being shed, not as much by Mrs. Cittone as by Mike and Linda. Both cried outright and comforted each other in their moment of grief.

Frank escorted the mother home, Mike did so for Linda. Next day mom was escorted by Frank again and Mike did so for Linda for the Mass, cemetery, and a lunch afterwards. When all functions were complete, Mike escorted Linda home, they embraced, and made plans to have dinner soon. After a few weeks they did so, and they repeated this once a week for two months. At first what they had in common was the loss of one they both loved. Although this loss persisted, they now realized the void created by Damon's demise was now being filled by each other's presence. When they finally realized that other feelings now existed between them, neither hesitated to make them known. They dated, introduced each to families, and they admitted to each other the love that existed between them, which brought up the obvious question. "What would Damon think?" It was first posed by Linda. Mike could only answer, "What would Damon think knowing we were both happy?" After thinking for a minute about this, they both knew the answer.

After continued togetherness for one more month, another obvious question had to arise. They sort of both hinted at a life with each other, and they agreed to become engaged in a month or less. Before a month elapsed, Mike Sampson gave an engagement ring to Linda D'Joseph and asked her to marry. She consented and kissed him and hugged him as hard as she could. She then told him what had been on her mind these last few months.

"I need to tell you something important Mike." "What is it Lin? You can tell me anything. I love you," responded Mike.

"Have you noticed anything about me Mike? Look at me." "You were thinner, I guess. But I love the way you are. I like some meat." "You know Mike," answered Lin, "Damon may be dead, but not all of him." "What do you mean?" said Mike. "You know Damon, and I were in love before he passed?" "Yes, I gathered that," answered Mike. "Well, we proved it as well. It was almost love at first sight. He admitted he adored my face with grease on it while trying to change a tire. I admitted I adored his manner and manliness while getting me to safety on a busy road. As I said, we were in love. And made love. I'm five months pregnant." There was a brief silence. Mike looked at her, took her in his arms and said, "I still love you. Both of you." He kissed Linda long and hard. After a minute Mike asked, "How did it happen?" Linda answered smiling, "It all began with a hockey game."

Part II
Chapter 14
It's a small world

In 1991 the state courthouse in Hazelton was over 150 years old. Besides various courtrooms on the main floor, there existed an ample amount of conference rooms, offices, and makeshift classrooms in the level below the first floor. They were used for legal conferences, judges and attorney's offices, and instruction rooms for junior staff employees of the courthouse such as law clerks, interns, paralegals, office and administrative employees, and all new hires. On a cold Saturday morning in January of that year that saw the start of the successful conclusion of the first Gulf War, the beginning years of Seinfeld and Law and Order on T.V., Rocky still punching in the movies, the S.F. 49ers with Steve Young on top in the NFL, Wayne Gretzsky the best in the NHL as was Michal Jordan in the NBA, one of these classrooms was filled with twenty students taking their final test to qualify for the battery of tests required to pass the bar in the Commonwealth of Pa. This was given only to those that successfully passed all preceding tests and requirements necessary to reach this final level. Monitoring this test was judge of the superior court of the state of Pa, Judge Francis Joseph Papal. When all were seated and preliminary instructions given, roll call was taken starting with A's. The judge began, "Abbott, Abertson, Andrews, Baily, Benson, Bonn, Canton, Cittone Jr., Davis, Devlin..." The judge hesitated and repeated, "Cittone," and a slim, curly-haired, fairly good-looking young man asked, "What's up judge? I said present when you said my name before." The face was even more familiar than the name. "Sorry" said the judge, "just wanted to know if I said it correctly." "You did" returned the youngster, and roll call was completed to Zachary.

The first hour of the three-hour exam was uneventful, but ten minutes into the second hour the judge noticed one student getting a little too cozy with his neighbor's exam paper. From his roll call paper, the judge saw the curious student was Albert Canton, seated beside Cittone. The judge quietly strolled next to Albert, informed him he witnessed plagiarism twice from Cittone's paper, and advised Mr. Canton to soon inform the powers that be that the judge excused him from this final because of sickness, and advised him to apply to retake the test the following month when it is given next. "Or would you rather I inform them of the real reason for your early exit from this classroom?" "No, no judge" interjected the stunned student, "Let's do it your way," agreed the thankful youngster, "I'll apply for next month's test," he continued, as he packed up and quickly vacated the premises.

Their volume was low enough not to disturb the class, but the exact nature of the brief dialogue was not lost on student Cittone.

At the end of the period, when all papers were handed in, the judge asked Mr. Cittone to remain for a minute. When they were alone in the room, the judge spoke firmly but carefully to the student. "I know you know what occurred with your buddy Albert, and I can't say I saw any cooperation on your part. I can also surmise by glancing at your paper that you did better than passing. So, I'm going to ignore any thoughts of cheating or assisting on your part. However, I want you to promise to help student Canton to pass when he tries again." He does so. "Do I have your word?" Mr. Cittone thought fast, and knew he better agree with this line of thinking, and said sharply, "No problem, sir, he will pass next month." "Good" replied the judge. "And if you are who I think you are, your word is enough." The young lawyer thought quickly again, "Who do you think I am?" he questioned. "Is you mother's name Linda, and your father's deceased around the early sixties?" The young man looked hard at him. The judge continued, "And your dad's best friend is named Mike, your grandmother is Sarah Cittone, if she's alive, and your dad was the most admired man I've ever known." "Ok judge, if you're finished with my history, tell me, who the heck are you, pardon the expression?" "I was a close friend of your father, and his lawyer a long time ago. I sat with your grandmother at Dad's funeral. Please tell your mother and grandmother Frank Papal was asking about them."

The youngster stuck out his hand saying, "Please to meet you sir." The judge gripped firmly "Same here son," and half hugged the student. The judge was pleased to be told that Mike was the young man's stepfather and had been married to his mom for almost 27 years. He told Judge Frank how both parents pushed him towards education, and also into organized sports from an early age. He was one of the starting pitchers for his high school, he said. When he didn't know what to do in college, both parents suggested pre-law, since he seemed to like people, and in fact belonged to volunteer Church and civic groups for poor and disabled. Young Damon also tutored students having trouble with school at his former H.S. The judge turned around for a few seconds and rubbed his eyes, saying to himself "The apple doesn't fall far..." He said he loved Mike as much as his mother, and also had a brother that was two years younger. They belonged to the same charity groups. The boy was puzzled by the judge's next question. "Do you have many mirrors in your house?" Young Damon said, "Come again."

The judge repeated. Damon, raising his eyebrows, said, "Yeah, in the bathroom to shave and comb hair. How many do you have judge?" The judge laughed. "The same" he answered. Still looking funny at the judge, he continued. "Funny you should ask that. My theory is mirrors are necessary, but put little stock in them. If you want to see how the world sees you, mirrors are close, not exact. Everything's reversed. Your right is the mirrors left, and vice versa, and you can only use one at a time, anyway. Why the heck do you ask?" "I just have odd curiosities," claimed the judge, thinking of something entirely different. The judge was satisfied with his answer. Damon Cittone Jr. was more satisfied with his own answer.

They spoke a few minutes longer, recalling each had commitments, and before parting the judge offered to take the new lawyer to dinner at his favorite eatery for his favorite dish.

He wanted to know more about Damon Jr. and his family and would relate all he knew of Damon's dad.

The following weekend they met at an expensive sea food restaurant which had the freshest shellfish of the five surrounding counties, and the prices reflected this. After a sumptuous meal of lobster tail with all the fixings, they spoke at length over coffee and dessert. Damon told how any values he learned were primarily from both parents. They were happy together, and they assisted him with his goals in life. Damon was told how his dad helped the judge when he was a young lawyer, and the things he learned from his dad. He said, "Your father based everything on commonsense. For instance, when you have a troubled client, if you really want to help, and get referrals for new clients, put yourself in the troubled person's shoes. Now, beside the legalities, you know how to deal with the client. Other things that have nothing to do with law. He'd say every A.M. you awake, look skyward and be thankful. Every night prior to retiring, look skyward again, and think whether you did any good in between. If you sleep well, then...well you get the picture, right Damon? And one that made me laugh, his horizontal promise theory. A promise's value is directly proportional with the angle your body forms with the ground or the horizon when making the promise. At 0° you're laying down and there's little or no value. Standing straight up at 90°is maximum value. An example is lying down with the opposite sex saying I'll give you the moon. And if you're touching while laying down, any promises have less than zero value." The boy listened intently, "And he never broke a promise. His word was gold. It showed at his funeral. The total that attended his funeral was the most that came to Carton Funeral Home since the mayor of the city died in office fifty-years ago." They sat silently for a minute or two. "I'm sure I've left out some pertinent info about dad, but I will recall it sooner or later. Meanwhile, if you're finished, we'll leave, and I want to invite you soon to my home for a beer maybe or pizza or whatever, and we can continue the confab. And soon I'd like to invite your parents also, let them know Damon." Judge Frank paid the bill, they said goodbyes and parted.

A few days later, Damon got a call inviting him to the judge's home for a brunch on the following Sunday, and young Damon accepted. He arrived around 11 A.M. and had a coffee with his friend and his gracious wife. They showed pictures of a son and daughter and their young families. He asked young Damon if he had a girl or wife. He said he's been seeing someone for six months, and they may become one. No rush by either of them. "How'd you meet?" asked the judge. "I helped her with a flat tire once." Damon looked squarely at the judge, started smiling, and then broke out laughing. "Gotcha, didn't I judge?" "Yeah, I guess you did," replied Judge Frank. "I talk to my mother about my father. She's always telling me something. Oh, I met JoAnn at work. She also belongs to one of our volunteer groups and I coach the softball team. I may play ball again myself. Right now, I'm too busy. Like I say, no rush. Anything else you remember about my pop, Judge?" queried young Damon. "As a matter of fact, I do," he answered. "He had a theory about addiction, be it drugs, alcohol, whatever. He used to say addicts should be given the harshest treatment possible at rehab. They should walk on nails, on fire, stay underwater until the last second and be subject to severe cold with just shorts on. And if they're still addicted afterward, you'll know the treatment wasn't strong enough. If they say they can't stop craving, they will stop while doing these tortuous activities. If they repeat the activities, they'll stop craving again. And if someone asks why so rough with the treatment, your answer is "It's not as rough as the effort required to break the habit."

"He encouraged people to try something if they thought they could do it. His logic was there was a good chance that others have succeeded at it with less talent."

"Did he believe in religion Judge?" asked the youngster.

"You know, I really don't know. He may have" answered Judge Frank "I know what he used to say. It went something like, the closest you'll ever get to God, if there is one, is as close as the person that's next to you. He would say, as far as miracles, I can see why God got out of that business. After all the miracles he performed, did the people get better, stop sinning, help each other? Not even close. They probably got worse. That's why there won't be any more miracles anytime soon."

They drank coffee and thought to themselves. Finally, the Judge asked, "What have you been doing lately? And how did you reach this point?" "Oh, let's see," replied young Damon, "After H.S. I did four years of pre-law, finished law school at 25, then was a law clerk at the big law firm Thomas and Thomas Inc. in town. They thought I should try to pass the bar, and I've been wanting to try.

So, I met you, judge. By the way, what weakness did my father have, while we're on the subject; we all have some."
"Well, I guess we all do," he came back. "Let's see, well, he might do a little daydreaming but nothing serious, he liked sex and enjoyed it, but that was only before he met your mother. He was also an employee of the month a few times, but that's not a fault. I just remembered it." He hesitated.
Damon came back "Anything else judge?" The judge had a thoughtful look on his face, "No, young Damon, it's all I remember," lied the Senior Sitting Judge of Superior Court of the Commonwealth of Pennsylvania.

The young man seemed satisfied, told the judge he should be going, that he had tickets for a local ball game that evening, and if he'd like to attend. The judge declined, saying he was tied up. The young man left, still concentrating on the many people helped by his dad, and the numerous friends he made during his short life. Young Damon thanked the judge, turned and grasped the doorknob to leave. He had the door half open, still wondering about his father, and the many he helped and saved from misery. He was proud to be his son. While young Damon was opening the front door, the judge got a call and asked the young man to wait a minute. He did. The judge hung up and said in a firm but friendly tone, "Damon, before you leave" he began, "There's a favor I'd like to ask you. There's a close friend of mine that said he may visit tonight, and he just confirmed it. I've been trying to advise him during a dark period of his life. Personal problems, wife problems, financial problems, and God knows what else. I'm almost at my wits end. He'll be here at seven tonight for another advice seminar from me. Do you think you could stop by then, and possibly give your opinion regarding his dilemmas, and offer any solutions to ease his heavy heart? I know it's an imposition. But isn't everything that's worthwhile? Whadaya say?" The judge waited for a response. The one he got took him back twenty-eight years, to a small room, in a small street, in a small town. Damon Cittone Jr., strolling slowly thru the doorway with his back to the judge froze momentarily, nodded his head and gave a high thumbs-up, raised seven fingers over his shoulders, went out and shut the door.

Chapter 15
Softball and a new friend

"Play ball," screamed the chunky umpire at 5:05 PM on a Friday afternoon at the softball field in the cities multi-sports complex on a warm sunny June day. Games were scheduled to start at 5PM sharp and last six innings or 'til 7PM, whichever came first. Any tie scores would remain so. All umps wanted to complete games and therefore pushed for a prompt start. The Downtown Doubles were hosting North End Sluggers in the first under 30 league regular season game. The first batter for the Sluggers was Simpson to be followed by Lane and Callahan Jr. Simpson hit a hard grounder to short and was thrown out on a close play at first. Lane worked the count full after fouling off three pitches. His fourth foul was in play and caught for the second out. Callahan went to the plate looking confident and hitterish. This attitude was not lost on Downtown's pitcher, and he kept most pitches outside the dish, and gave up a walk. Hitting cleanup was left fielder Jake Duchene, and he looked the part at 6 ft. 1 in. tall and 250 lbs. Pitcher Sammy Camper was about to depend on his breaking ball and change up to fool the big guy. The first three breakers resulted in a 2-1 count. Next was an outside strike to even the count. Then a high foul out of play. Sammy was going for the payoff. A good time to try an inside fastball was his guess. He whipped it to the plate and Jake lifted a very high fly to left, and the fielder ran to his right to make the play. Reaching his right hand out as far as he could, the Downtown fielder caught the drive, but a second later tripped on some bad turf and committed an error and dropped it. Runners now on second and third because of Callahan thinking there was only one out and not running at full speed.

"Ha, what's up buddy? Come to visit?" joked third basemen Cittone Jr. at base runner Callahan. "Shouldn't you be home by now? Your buddies on the bench look like they were expecting you." "I know, I know, I wasn't paying attention. I'll get there." "Confident dude, eh?" countered Cittone. "We'll see." Next batter walked. Batter #7 grounded to third and Cittone fielded it and threw home behind an overconfident Callahan. A second before Callahan hit the plate, catcher Phil Savarese's glove hit his shin holding onto the ball. Runner Callahan screamed at third basemen Cittone, "Why didn't you go to first?" "Shorter throw pal," the fielder came back. "Bullshit," Callahan uttered to himself. "Everybody goes to first on grounders," thought the runner.

"O.K. get ready guys," hollered Coach Sanders to the Downtown Doubles. "This pitcher is good, but we're better. Swing only at the good ones." First batter Adams lifted a fly to center that was caught easily. Next hitter hit a fly to short left field, which fell between left fielder Duchene and shortstop Callahan. Man on first, one out. Third batter Cittone worked the count full, then grounded sharply to short. Callahan scooped it, flipped to second and watched the throw to first finish the double play. The shortstop smiled at runner Cittone. "Revenge is sweet, but quick revenge is delicious," thought Jimmy Callahan

Jr. Runner Cittone laughed to himself and thought to himself, "Next time."

As the game progressed, each pitcher had a 2-hitter and a shutout. Top of the sixth. Lane was up for the Sluggers. After a 1-1 count he hit a hard grounder to third, fielded by Cittone on a diving play. But by the time he got in position to throw an out was doubtful. A very quick Lane beat out a good throw by Cittone for an infield hit. Third batter Callahan came to the plate. He smiled at third. The third basemen did likewise. First was a called strike, then 2 balls. 2 ground fouls outside the third base line caused right fielder Richman to move toward center about 15 ft., leaving right kind of empty. Noticing the move, Callahan shifted his left foot a little toward right field and his right foot a little farther from the dish. Next pitch crossed the outside of the plate before it was lofted to right about 10 ft. from the foul line. Richman playing too far to his right had no hope of catching it. Lane, with a good lead off first, zoomed around second heading to third with no intention of stopping. Rounding third he knew it would be close at home and prepared his slide. The second baseman took the relay, threw home and the catcher tagged Lane a split second after he scored. 1-0, Sluggers were up. No outs. Callahan on second. Next batter, cleanup guy lifted a deep fly to the right which was caught. One out. Callahan tug up and slid into third and on a close play was safe. "We have to stop meeting like this," chuckled third batter Cittone. "I won't be here long," returned runner Callahan. "We'll see," Damon shot back. Fifth batter grounded to first for the second out. Batter number 6 walked. 2 outs. Men on first and third. Seventh batter fouled off four times before he also took a walk. Loaded with 2 down. Eighth batter took four practice swings before stepping in the box. He looked hitterish. First was a called strike. Next was a foul behind the plate. 0-2. Then 2 balls. At 2-2, the pitcher felt it was time for his spinner. This thing spun so fast that if it is hit it usually only pops up or is a grounder. The pitch came. The batter saw it and hit a sharp grounder to third. Cittone fielded it going hard to his left and going to his knees. Knowing he's too far from the bag, he swiped at the runner going to third with his gloved hand and hit the runner's calf.

Ump made the "out" call and ended the inning. Bottom of the sixth coming. 1-0 slugs.

Batter #9 was up for Downtown. He fanned. Batter Adams fouled off a dozen before walking. Lane worked a full count before lining a rope to deep left. It bounded off the wall before it was caught and thrown well to third to hold and stop the run. Lane slid into second on the throw. 1 out, men on second and third. Batter Cittone stepping in, smiled and looked confident. "Gimme something to clean the bases," he joked to the catcher. First pitch was a swinging strike. Then 2 balls and 2 high fouls out of play. 2 and 2, 1 away. Next pitch was a little low, but only a little outside the middle of the dish. Damon saw it well, and it was just what he needed for at least a sac fly. He swung a little under center and sent a high fly to deep left. Both runners tagged up knowing it could be caught, and it was with a diving catch against the fence. Runner No. 5 on third easily scored, and man on second, fast lane Eddie, as he was called, slid into third in a cloud of dust, almost blinding third basemen Lane who took the relay but couldn't find the runner in the dust storm around the bag.

Tie score, man on third, 2 outs. Cleanup hitter stepped in the box, swinging hard and fast and looking like what he was, a big strong cleanup slugger. Noticing these actions, the infield quickly backed up, and the outfield followed suit. First pitch was a ball. Next came a deep fly in foul territory that was out of play. Another ball. The 2-1 pitch that followed was a slow curve that curved only half as much as it should. Fielders felt this would be smacked and fell back a step. The cleanup man prepared to swing, then lowered the bat across the plate and bounced a soft bunt down the first base line. It was fair by a foot and a half but was heading foul.

He tore down the line for the bag and noticed half the infield charging the ball. The first baseman finally fielded it and threw to the second basemen covering, but it was a split second after the runner crossed the bag and the man from third scored.

Cheers and screaming filled the air as the ump signaled safe for both runners and the game was over at 6:55 PM. Even the ump was happy. The teams shook hands and a few of the sluggers commented on the bunting strategy. "It was Cittone's idea" they said. Young Damon related how he learned it from his dad when the elder Cittone sometimes coached a team for a close friend who was busy with family problems. "Great idea" the Sluggers admitted. "Yeah, it was" agreed young Damon. "I learned a lot of great things from my pop, considering I never knew him. But I met his closest friends as I grew up, and they pretty much filled me in." "Good game guys," the Sluggers concluded and went on their way. Except one. Callahan came over to congratulate the team and lingered for a minute or two with Cittone. "I still say you throw to first with two outs at all times." Jimmy was serious but smiling. "Most of the time," countered Cittone. Callahan studied Damon for a second or two. Damon laughed, "What are you going to do, punch me?" Jimmy Jr. laughed, "No, not at all pal. I was just thinking, maybe I'll buy you a beer sometime. You know, just drink and bullshit for a while. Who knows? Maybe we'll have more in common than just softball. Whadaya say?" Damon considered, "Ok, why not. But I'll buy next time."

Chapter 16
Does the end justify the means?

Two days later Damon Cittone Jr. met Jimmy Callahan Jr. at a neighborhood bar that they both frequented. After greeting each other, they settled at the bar for beer and pretzels and decided to split a super roast beef hoagie that could satisfy two easily. "Well Jimmy, since you called this meeting, tell me what's up with Jimmy Callahan Jr. Then I'll tell you what's up with me," started Damon Jr. "Ah, I guess not much really." answered Jimmy. "I work for a plumber and just finished being an apprentice and am a journeyman at this time. It's hard sometimes, but it's good work and I learn a lot. I'm interested in it. That's what really matters. My father got me the job. He's a police inspector. Been a cop for almost 30 years. Has a lot of friends. I also work part time at my father's center downtown." "What's it called?" asked Damon. "Jimmy Cal's Youth Development Center" returned Jimmy. "Oh, I heard of that," said Damon. "Is that the one that helps homeless youngsters and poor ones throughout the city?" "The same," returned Jimmy. "And I give them free plumbing." "Why not?" said Damon. "Hey that place helps a lotta kids," returned Damon. "Isn't that the place that saved that kid from flunking his senior year at the high school? And the place that gave money to the girl for college supplies cause she was from a poor family?" "That's two of them Damon. But it's more like two hundred we've assisted since it opened 15 years ago.

But before all that happens, we must perform the required day-to-day duties that are the foundation of the center. Our people assist the youngsters in any facet of their lives that's giving them trouble. We teach job and trade skills, home making chores, academic subjects, small business skills and family and social life. And anything else they can come up with. We have two classrooms for academics, job and life skills and business operations. There's also two lab type rooms for trades and home making classes. Each youngster is given an outline of what is taught in each class and the frequency and length of the course they seem interested in. If they don't know what to join, we advise them accordingly based on background, age, sex, and intelligence. Once they start a course, they must complete it. If they drop it prematurely without a very valid reason, they're gone. They can re-apply after a year, but we are not obligated to enroll them. And I neglected to mention that when anyone first joins J.C.'s center, they must sign a waiver that prevents them bringing any type of lawsuit against the center or its staff for any reason, be it information, demonstrations, or advice of any kind that they feel was harmful to them. In times like these, you can't be too careful. After all, they're getting this advice and two medium size meals a day for free. When this is pointed out to new members, most sign up. If any are of an age that requires a parent or guardian's signature, of which many are, we get that signature as well. And we also include the 'YW' and 'YMCA' in our protection waiver. We don't want to be a thorn in their side after helping us with our facilities and operations."

"The center is now under the direction of the YW and YMCA and we must follow their rules and regs. But we take it much further that the "Y." Besides their rules, our people must follow ours. No drugs, booze, criminal activity of any kind and no gang activity. We don't care what young males and females did prior to joining our organization. If they truly want to develop into fine men and women socially, academically, financially, and aim toward a responsible career in a profession, trade or business, we will assist them in any way possible, consistent with whatever finances their families have or do not have. However, if they violate any of our rules or the Y's, they are out. No second chances. And they're quite plainly informed of this upon joining with their applications. There are just too many trying to get into Jimmy Cal's, and we can't have any bottlenecks holding up any deserving youngsters. We have assisted a couple hard cases in the past, but these were special circumstances, and these couple were told to keep their problems under their hats so we could assist them, very unofficially. We've had citations and awards from two State Governors of PA, and even got into TIME Magazine once and The New York Times once, in addition to our local papers. So, you see Damon, this is nothing to mess with, as my dad would say. And I'll likely take it over when my dad is too tired or too old. So, now you know the story of J.C. Youth Center."

"I sure do" exclaimed Damon. "How did your dad get to open a place like that?" inquired Damon seriously. "Well, like I said" answered Jimmy, "he's a cop, has many friends, and got contributions from a good bit of them, as I understand. Used his own money as well. Wants to give back to the community, he always says. Licensing was no problem since he knows everyone in the city government. But it's all up and up. 'Wouldn't want it any other way' he always says. He's been helped, so he wants to return the favor." "How's he been helped?" asked Damon. "Well, the biggest way I know of," starts Jimmy, "was when I was little, around 2 or 3 years old. I had a growth in my head that turned malignant and needed removal. It also needed money. Big operation. Big money. Something about less insurance coverage than this required. Anyway, some people helped him out, financially I guess, and I got surgery. Everything worked out well. I get headaches occasionally, but they go away. I also was told it affected my behavior when I was little. But I'm ok now." "You seem fine to me, Jim" agreed Damon. "Except for maybe always throwing to first base," quipped Damon.

They smiled at this. "Who was this person or persons that helped your dad?" asked Damon. "No idea," said Jimmy. "It's all hush-hush if you speak to my father. 'No need to dig up old stones' he says. But he claims he returned the favor. He helped the family of the one that helped him most. Got them started with housing and some used furniture when they were starting out. 'Goodwill cribs are just as good as new ones' he would say." "Hey, I had one of them," Damon said sharply. "So did I" returned Jimmy. "We didn't always have money,' continued Jimmy Jr. "What about you Damon? What's up with you pal?" "Not much, really. I work, play ball, have a girlfriend, a mother and stepfather that is as close as a real father as possible. I'll give you details next time Jimmy, when I buy the beers."

"But what makes you think we got more in common?" "I don't know, just a feeling I guess," returned Callahan.

Damon Jr. smiled at his competitor. "You know why you don't always throw to first with 2 outs? Because you don't always do a lot of things 'all the time,' nothing to do with baseball. It's life. Yeah, I think I will buy you a beer." continued Damon. "You're on Damon," answered little Jimmy. "But don't be disappointed if we have little more in common," finished Damon. "You never know," answered Callahan. "I guess not," returned Cittone. "But I can't imagine what." As they both turned to leave the bar and go their separate ways, young Damon called to the other sharply. "Well, as my father used to say, 'see you later alligator'." Little Jimmy came back more sharply. "And as my father used to say, 'after while crocodile'."

www.ingramcontent.com/pod-product-compliance
Lightning Source LLC
La Vergne TN
LVHW091031150826
845672LV00006BA/1761

* 9 7 9 8 8 4 4 1 6 1 6 0 5 *